MISSOURI MADHOUSE

Here's what readers from around the country are saying about Johnathan Rand's *AMERICAN CHILLERS:*

"Your books are awesome! I have all the
AMERICAN CHILLERS and I keep them right
by my bed since I read them every week!"
-Tommy W, age 9, Michigan

"My dog chewed up TERRIBLE TRACTORS OF TEXAS,
and then he puked. Is that normal?"
-Carlos V., age 11, New Jersey

"Johnathan Rand's books are my favorite.
They're really creepy and scary!"
-Jeremy J., age 9, Illinois

"My whole class loves your books! I have two
of them and they are really, really cool."
-Katie R., age 12, California

"I never liked to read before, but now I read
all the time! The 'Chillers' series is great!"
-Lauren B., age 10, Ohio

"I love AMERICAN CHILLERS because they
are scary, but not too scary, because I don't want
to have nightmares."
-Adrian P., age 11, Maine

"I just finished Florida Fog Phantoms.
It is a freaky book! I really liked it."
-Daniel R., Michigan

"I read all of the books in the MICHIGAN CHILLERS series, and I just started the AMERICAN CHILLERS series. I really love these books!"
-*Andrew K., age 13 Montana*

"I have six CHILLERS books, and I have read them all three times! I hope I get more for my birthday. My sister loves them, too."
-*Jaquann D., age 10, Illinois*

"I just read KREEPY KLOWNS OF KALAMAZOO and it really freaked me out a lot. It was really cool!"
-*Devin W., age 8, Texas*

"THE MICHIGAN MEGA-MONSTERS was great! I hope you write lots more books!"
-*Megan P., age 12, Kentucky*

"All of my friends love your books! Will you write a book and put my name in it?"
-*Michael L., age 10, Ohio*

"These books are the best in the world!"
-*Garrett M., age 9, Colorado*

"We read your books every night. They are really scary and some of them are funny, too."
-*Michael & Kristen K., Michigan*

"I read THE MICHIGAN MEGA-MONSTERS in two days, and it was cool! When are you going to write one about Wisconsin?"
-*John G., age 12, Wisconsin*

"Johnathan Rand is my favorite author!"
-Kelly S., age 8, Michigan

"AMERICAN CHILLERS are great. I got one
for Christmas, and I loved it. Now, my sister
is reading it. When she's done, I'm going to
read it again."
-Joel F., age 13, New York

"I like the CHILLERS books because they are
fun to read. They are scary, too."
-Hannah K., age 11, Minnesota

"I read the MEGA-MONSTERS book and I
really liked it. Mr. Rand is a great writer."
-Ryan M., age 12, Arizona

"I LOVE AMERICAN CHILLERS!"
-Zachary R., age 8, Indiana

"I read your book to my little sister and
she got freaked out. I did, too!"
-Jason J., age 12, Ohio

"These books are my favorite! I love reading them!"
-Sarah N., age 10, New Jersey

"Your books are great. Please write more so I can read them."
-Dylan H., age 7, Tennessee

#10: Missouri Madhouse

Johnathan Rand

An AudioCraft Publishing, Inc. book

Graphics layout/design consultant: Scott Beard, Straits Area Printing
Honorary graphics consultant: Chuck Beard *(we miss you, Chuck)*
Editor: Diane Gurnee

Book warehouse and storage facilities provided by Clarence and Dorienne's Storage, Car Rental & Shuttle Service, Topinabee Island, MI
Security provided by Salty and Abby.

ISBN 1-893699-50-1

Printed in USA

First Printing, July 2003

Missouri
Madhouse

Visit the official 'American Chillers' web site at:

www.americanchillers.com

Featuring excerpts from upcoming stories, interviews, contests, official American Chillers wearables, and *more!* Plus, join the FREE American Chillers fan club!

My name is Amber DeBarre, and if you're reading this, there's a pretty good chance that you're a friend of mine.

Because I don't want just *anyone* reading about the things that happened to us. I wrote this down so I would always remember what happened to me . . . and to share what happened with good friends.

I live near in Blue Springs, Missouri. They call Missouri the 'show me' state. And while I can't really 'show you' what happened, I can *tell* you all about it.

And I will tell you right off: what you're about to read isn't just an *ordinary* spooky story. In fact, if you frighten easily, you may not want to read this at all.

It all started one Friday night last summer. We live outside of the city where there are a lot of farms and old homes. My friend, Courtney Richards, lives about a mile south of us. She and her family just moved to Blue Springs, but we became best friends right away. She's eleven, just like me, and we're both in the same class at school.

On this particular evening, Courtney was coming to my house to spend the night. We switch every few weeks. I'll stay over at her house one time, and she'll stay at mine the next. We always have a lot of fun. We usually stay up late and watch scary movies on television.

Her parents dropped her off at seven o'clock. We ate popcorn and started to watch a scary movie in our basement. That's kind of our 'play' room. We have a big TV, a pool table, and a computer with a bunch of games. Whenever we have guests over, or when Courtney comes to spend the night, we hang out in the play room.

"This movie is *sooooo* boring," Courtney said as she shoved a handful of popcorn into her mouth. "It's not even scary."

"I know," I said. "They sure don't make them like they used to. Remember the last one we saw?"

"You mean *'Revenge at Camp Creepy'?*"

"Yeah," I said with a shudder. "Now *that* was a scary movie!"

We watched for a few more minutes, but the movie just got worse.

"Geez," Courtney said. "This show is just *bad*. I want something that is *really* scary."

"I know of a *place* that's really scary," I said.

"You do? Really?" Courtney's eyes were wide. The television chattered on, but neither of us were paying any attention to it anymore.

"Yeah," I replied. "It's a house not too far from here. Have you ever heard of 'The Madhouse'?"

Courtney thought about it for a moment, then shook her head. "No, I haven't."

"It's not far from here. Nobody goes there anymore."

"Why?" she asked.

"Well . . . they just don't. They're afraid to."

"How about you?" Courtney asked. "Are you afraid to?"

I paused for a moment. I didn't want to tell Courtney the truth.

Because the truth was, I was more than just afraid of the old place everyone called 'The Madhouse'.

I was terrified. But I just couldn't tell Courtney that.

"Oh, it scares *some* people," I said. "But not me."

"Take me there!" she said, her eyes shining with excitement.

I looked at the clock on the wall. It was eight o'clock, and it wouldn't be getting dark for almost two hours.

"Well . . ." I said.

"Unless you're afraid to," Courtney challenged.

"What?" I replied. "Me? Afraid? No way. We can go right now if you want."

"I want!" she said, jumping to her feet. Her blonde hair bounced around her shoulders. "A spooky old home! This is going to be *kew*-wool!" That's how Courtney pronounces the word *cool*, and when she's *really* excited, she says it a *lot*.

Unfortunately, it wasn't going to be cool.

It was going to be terrifying.

2

The place we call 'The Madhouse' isn't far from where we live. It's at the end of an old dirt road. There are no other houses around it, and not many people have a reason to travel the road.

I told Courtney what I knew about the place as we walked.

"It's been there as long as I can remember," I said. "No one has lived there in a long, long time."

"So?" Courtney said. "There are lots of houses like that all over the place. Is it haunted?"

"Well, I don't know if you could say if it was haunted or not," I replied. "It looks really creepy, like a big face."

"The house has a face?!?!" Courtney said.

"Well, sort of," I replied. "When you see it, you'll know what I mean. And strange things have happened there."

"Like what?"

"Well, a long time ago, a boy used to live there with his family. But he never went outside."

"He stayed in the house?" Courtney asked.

I nodded. "That's what everyone says. They say that he never, ever left the house. Not once."

"What happened to him?" Courtney asked.

"Nobody knows," I replied. "But people say that he was really sad. They say that sometimes, if you look really close, you can still see him in the house. All you have to do is look into the windows."

"What do you see in the windows?" Courtney asked.

"Different people see different things, I guess," I replied. "But a lot of people say that they've seen a boy in the window. They say that he waves at them and wants them to come inside."

"That's weird," Courtney said.

"I know," I agreed.

"Have you ever seen anything in the windows?"

Should I tell her? I wondered. *Should I tell her what I saw last year?*

No.

I didn't want to lie to my friend . . . it's just that . . . well . . . I guess I'm not exactly sure *what* I saw.

"Let's just say that there is something weird going on at the house," I said. "I *know* there is."

Courtney shivered and giggled. "Kew-*wool!*" she said. "A real spookhouse! This will be a lot more fun than watching a dumb movie on television!"

"A *Madhouse*," I corrected her. "Everyone calls it the Madhouse."

The evening air was chilly. Both of us were wearing sweatshirts, and I was glad—because I noticed that as we got closer to the old house, the temperature seemed to drop even further. A cold wind grazed my cheeks.

The sun dipped below the trees and we walked in the shadows of giant oaks and maples. Goldenrod grew thick along the side of the road.

Up ahead, at the end of the street, the Madhouse came into view.

"There it is," I whispered.

"Wow," Courtney said. "It *does* look like a face."

The two-story home sat in the shade of the trees. Its windows were dark and forbidding–cold, empty eyes that seemed to watch your every move. The wooden siding was gray and weathered, like the wrinkled skin of an old hag. The front yard was overgrown with tall, sinewy grass.

"Somebody should fire the groundskeeper," Courtney said. "That guy hasn't done anything."

I laughed. Just the thought of a groundskeeper working at the Madhouse seemed funny.

Suddenly, I felt a chill go through my body. I wondered if it was just the wind. I didn't *feel* cold . . . but I shivered just the same. And as we drew closer to the house, I began to feel more and more uneasy.

I had good reason to, as we were about to find out.

3

We stopped directly in front of the house, standing at the edge of the dirt road. The tall, uncut grass brushed against our legs. A locust sang from a nearby tree, buzzing like a high-tension electrical wire.

Once again, that same chill swept through my body. Suddenly, I didn't want to be there. I didn't want to be there *at all*. I wanted to be home, in our playroom, watching a scary movie on television, even if it *was* goofy. I wanted to turn and run . . . but I didn't.

"Wow," Courtney whispered. *"It looks even spookier from here."*

I pointed to the windows. "See how dark they are?" I said. "Some people say that those windows are so black, you can't see any reflection."

"No!"

I bobbed my head. "Yep. They say that if you see anything at all, it's going to be something that is so weird that it will make you go mad."

"That's just plain silly," Courtney said. "I mean . . . the house looks creepy and all, but that just seems *silly*."

"Hey, that's what they say," I replied.

"Well, then, let's go see," Courtney said.

All the time we had been walking, I was hoping that Courtney wouldn't ask to get close to the house. I was hoping that she would see it, get spooked, and that would be enough. I didn't think that she would actually want to get close to the house and look into the windows.

Cold fear slithered through my brain as I looked at the house. The tall grass swayed gently, and a soft breeze purred through the trees.

"Well?" Courtney said.

I wanted to turn and run. I wanted to go home. I didn't want to be here.

And so, when I heard myself saying 'okay', I knew right away that I was making a big mistake.

We both were.

Without another word, we began to walk through the waist-high grass.

Toward the Madhouse.

"Wait!"

I grabbed Courtney's hand. She stopped and turned toward me.

"What is it?" Courtney asked.

"I . . . I just . . . oh, I don't know," I said. "It's silly."

"What?" Courtney asked. "What's silly?"

"I just feel . . . *weird*, I guess."

"You're right," Courtney said with a smile. She gave my hand a squeeze and let it go. "You *do* feel weird. Come on."

I took a breath, and we continued walking through the grass. The sun was dropping fast, but a few thin blades of light still knifed through the thick trees. It would be dark soon.

More locusts droned from the trees, and their buzzing drowned out all other sounds. The singing insects were so loud that I couldn't even hear our feet crunch through the tall grass.

"What do you think we'll see?" Courtney asked. She sounded excited, like this was just another adventure and she had nothing to fear.

I, however, knew better.

"Oh, I don't know," I replied, my eyes bouncing from one dark window to the next. "Probably nothing."

We were almost to the house. I was glad that it wasn't dark yet.

"See anything?" Courtney asked.

I shook my head. "Nope."

"We probably have to be closer," she said. "I think it would be cool to see something in the windows. Wouldn't that be spooky?"

"Yeah," I replied with a nervous laugh.

We stopped. Four old, rickety steps led up to the porch. The wood was gray and worn. I reached out and touched the railing. It felt gritty and dry beneath my fingers.

We craned our necks to see into the windows.

"They sure are dark," she said. I didn't respond. We stood there for a moment, looking up at the old home that loomed over us.

The Madhouse.

"Come on," I said after a few moments. "Let's go home before it gets dark."

"Just a minute," Courtney said, and she placed her right foot on the first step. Then she raised her left to the next. I stayed right where I was.

She looked back at me. "You're not coming?" she asked.

"I'm going to stay right here," I said.

"Fine with me," she replied. Then she took two more steps and was on the porch. Cautiously, she walked toward a window.

"I don't see anything," she said. "The window is really dark."

"Can you see inside?" I asked.

Courtney shook her head. "No. It's too dark. I can see my own reflection, though. I guess that means that I'm not a vampire."

29

I giggled. We watched a movie about vampires once, and we found out that vampires don't have a reflection in mirrors or glass.

Of course, vampires don't *really* exist, but we thought it was kind of funny anyway.

"There are some more windows on the side of the house," I said. "We can go look there."

Courtney shrugged. "Okay," she said. "But I don't see why they call this place the Madhouse. It doesn't look any different than any other old house."

She turned and stepped off the porch, and we waded through the tall grass to the side of the house. Here, the final rays of sun streamed through the trees, and I breathed a sigh of relief. It wasn't as dark on this side of the house.

We approached a window and stared at it. We could see our reflections clearly, but nothing else.

Courtney raised her hands, placed her thumbs in her ears, and wiggled her fingers. She stared at her own reflection in the window.

"Look!" she exclaimed, raising her eyebrows. "I'm a monster! Booga, booga!"

I laughed. She looked really silly.

"Booga, booga!" she said again, wiggling her fingers faster. I laughed at her reflection in the window. "See?" she said. "The Madhouse has made me crazy! Booga, booga!"

She stuck her tongue out and wagged it back and forth while she wiggled her fingers. I laughed so hard that tears came to my eyes.

"Booga, booga!" Courtney giggled, rolling her eyes. "Booga —"

Suddenly, Courtney stopped moving. She stopped speaking.

She had a strange look on her face, and she slowly lowered her hands. She squinted and peered into the window.

Her expression changed from curiosity to shock. Her head jerked back. I looked into the window.

Our faces reflected in the dark glass, but now we could see something else. At first it was fuzzy and murky, but as we watched, the image cleared.

Suddenly, I noticed that the forest around us had become very still and quiet. No locusts buzzed, no breeze whispered through the trees.

That familiar chill swept through me again, only stronger this time. My whole body tensed. I gasped. Courtney's mouth opened to scream, but no sound came out. There was *another* face in the window.

The face of a boy.

"Hey guys! What's up?"

I jumped nearly out of my skin and shrieked loudly. Courtney spun around. He had been behind us, and we saw his reflection in the window.

"Scott!" I scolded. "You scared us to death!"

He looked at me, then at Courtney. "You look pretty alive to me," he said.

Scott Palmer has been my friend for a long time. We're in the same grade, and we used to be in the same class. He lives a few houses away from us. He's the same height as me, and his brown hair is almost identical to the color of mine . . . except his is a lot shorter.

"I didn't mean to sneak up on you," he said. "I stopped by your house and your mom said that you had gone for a walk down here."

"Yeah, well, you surprised us all right," Courtney said. She'd met Scott a few times, but they didn't know each other real well.

"Checking out the Madhouse, huh?" he said, peering into the window. "See anything?"

"No," I replied, shaking my head.

"Nothing at all," Courtney said.

"Well, a lot of people have," Scott said. "My dad says there are a lot of weird things that happen at this house."

"I want to see something!" Courtney whined. "I really do!"

"You need to stare into the window for a long time," Scott said. "You can't just look into a window and look away. You really have to concentrate."

"Scott," I warned, "I don't think that's a good idea."

"All you have to do is just focus on one place in the glass," Scott continued, ignoring me. "Go ahead, Courtney. Try it."

"Scott!" I pleaded. "Don't—"

"Oh, come on, Amber," he said. "Don't be such a chicken."

"So, all I have to do is stare into the window?" Courtney asked. She glanced at her reflection in the glass, then turned to Scott.

"Yeah," he said. "But you really need to concentrate. Give it a try."

Courtney turned back toward the window. "Okay," she said.

I grabbed Scott by the arm and pulled. He walked with me to the front of the house, leaving Courtney standing before the window. We were far enough away so she couldn't hear us, but we stayed in a spot where we could see her.

"You shouldn't have told her that!" I hissed.

"What's the big deal, Amber?" he hissed back.

"The 'big deal' is that something is going on at this house," I whispered. *"Nobody knows what, but there is something going on here!"*

"Yeah, well, nobody has ever been hurt, have they?"

I glanced over at Courtney. She was a few feet away from the house, gazing into the window.

35

"No," I replied. *"Not yet."*

"Then quit your worrying," Scott whispered. *"Besides . . . she probably won't see anything, anyway."*

We watched Courtney for a moment. She continued to gaze into the window.

Finally, I walked back to her. "Come on, Court," I said. "Let's go home."

Courtney didn't say anything.

"Hey," I said, waving my hand in front of her face. "Come on. We don't have to watch that dumb scary movie. We can watch something else."

But Courtney didn't even blink. She didn't move or speak.

"Courtney?" I asked. "Courtney?"

Still, there was no response from her.

Suddenly, her eyes grew wide. I turned my head to look into the window, but I only saw my own reflection and Courtney's horrified expression glaring back at me.

Her mouth opened. Slowly, she raised her arm and pointed at the window.

And screamed.

Her screams echoed through the trees. A few birds, alarmed by the noise, screeched and flew off, their wings beating the air as they fled.

"Courtney!" I shouted.

Courtney stopped screaming and threw her hands over her face, covering her eyes. She turned away, gasping.

"It was horrible!" she choked. "Just horrible!"

By now, Scott had raced to her side.

"What did you see?!?!" he said.

Courtney's hands were still pressed to her face.

"I . . . I saw . . . I saw a . . . television set," she choked. "A scary movie was playing . . . but . . .

but it wasn't scary! It was silly . . . and we couldn't shut it off!"

"Really?!?!" Scott asked.

Suddenly, Courtney threw down her hands, revealing a sly smirk. "No!" she exclaimed. "Gotcha!" She laughed.

"Ooh, you!" I scolded. "You had me going!"

"Me too!" Scott said. "I really thought something was wrong!"

But it *was* kind of funny. Courtney would probably make a good actress.

"It's getting dark, guys," I said. " Scott . . . you want to come over and watch a scary movie?"

"I can't," Scott replied. "I'm supposed to get up early and help my dad haul some stuff to the junkyard."

"Too bad," Courtney said. "We've got a ton of popcorn."

We walked along the side of the house and into the front yard. The sun had gone down, and the trees were shadowy and still. The house was dark and silent. The locusts had stopped buzzing, and crickets had started to chirp.

"Some Madhouse," Courtney said. She turned and began to walk through the tall grass back to the dirt road. Scott and I followed.

"Well, there *are* strange things that happen here," I insisted. "Everybody knows about it."

"Amber is right," Scott said. "The Madhouse has a lot of freaky history."

"Sure," Courtney replied. "And pigs fly." She reached the road and turned, looking at the house. "I mean . . . it looks kind of spooky and all, but that's no big deal."

Scott and I reached the road and turned. The three of us were facing the house.

"Hey, you can ask my dad," Scott said. "He'll tell you."

"I've seen all I need to see," Courtney said. "It's just a big, dark, dumb house."

All at once there was a loud banging sound, causing the three of us to jump.

I took a cautious step back onto the dirt road, and so did Courtney and Scott.

"Did . . . did you guys see that?" Courtney asked. Her voice trembled with fear.

"I can't believe it," I said.

"Believe it," Scott said, and I could tell he was frightened. "I saw it, too."

On the front of the house, the window next to the front door had opened with such force that it should have shattered.

The window had opened all by itself!

7

"O . . . o . . . o . . . k . . . kay," Courtney stuttered. "I believe you guys. There is something weird going on at this house."

"*I told you,*" I whispered. "*This is why they call it the Madhouse. As a matter of fact, the same thing happened to me last year. I saw the window open by itself. I got scared and ran home.*"

"But there has to be *some* reason why that happened," Courtney said. "There has to be."

"Ghosts and spooks," Scott piped.

"There is no such thing," Courtney said defiantly. "Only in books and movies."

"Then how do you explain that?" I asked, pointing to the house. "That window opened all by itself!"

Courtney turned and faced us. It was getting dark quickly and I could barely make out her face in the murky gloom. "Suppose it didn't open all by itself," she said. "Maybe it's someone playing a joke on us. Maybe it's just you guys, trying to scare me!"

"What?!?!" I exclaimed. "Get real! How would we do that?! How could we open a window when we're this far away?"

"I don't know," Courtney replied with a confident smirk. "But I'm going to find out."

That being said, Courtney turned and began to walk through the tall grass.

Toward the Madhouse.

"What are you doing?!?!" Scott called out after her.

"I know what you two are up to," Courtney said without turning around. "You thought you'd get me back for scaring you when I was over by the window!"

"That's crazy!" I shouted.

"Oh yeah?" she replied. "Then how come you won't come with me to look at the window?"

"Because . . . because it's not safe," Scott said.

"You're just saying that to scare me," Courtney said. She stopped at the porch. We could barely see her in the late evening gloom. "You two are either trying to scare me, or you're just chickens. Which is it?"

"I'm no chicken," Scott said, and he started forward through the tall grass.

"*Scott!*" I hissed.

He kept walking, but he turned his head. "Well, I'm *not*," he said to me.

All right, I thought. *There are three of us. Nothing can happen. Nothing will happen. We can protect each other.*

I followed Scott through the field.

Nothing will happen, I reminded myself. *Nothing can happen.*

Wrong.

Sometimes, things *do* happen. *Scary* things. *Weird* things.

And they were about to.

I stopped at the porch where Scott and Courtney waited. We were only a few feet away from the open window.

"I dare you to stick your head inside the window," Courtney said to me.

"You're crazy," I replied.

"Maybe," she said. She looked at Scott. "How about you?"

"I'm not afraid," he replied, taking a step up onto the porch. Then he stopped and turned.

"All three of us together?" he said.

"Fine with me," Courtney said.

I knew it wasn't a good idea, but I went along with it.

"Okay," I said. "All three of us together. We'll look through the open window, and then we'll go home. Deal?"

"Deal," Scott and Courtney said at the same time.

The three of us walked up the steps and across the porch, stopping right in front of the window. By now, it was far too dark to see much of anything.

That's when the music started.

It sounded far away and dreamy, but it was definitely music.

Carnival music.

The three of us stood motionless. We all heard the strange sounds that seemed to be coming through the open window.

"It sounds like a fair," I whispered. *"It sounds like calliope music."*

And it did. The music sounded happy and fun and reminded me of the time the carnival came to town.

"Where's it coming from?" Scott asked quietly.

"It sounds like it's coming from inside," I said. *"From somewhere in the house."*

Slowly, the three of us leaned toward the window. The sound grew a little louder, but it was still quite faint.

We could see nothing but inky blackness. There were no lights in the house, of course, and as we peered through the window we could only see darkness.

Until—

We reached the window.

As we leaned closer to the open window, the music grew louder.

But the second that our heads poked *through* the open window, everything changed.

And at that moment, I knew that my life would never, ever be the same again.

What we were seeing wasn't the inside of a house.

We were looking at a carnival!

It was the most bizarre thing that had ever happened to me.

The instant our heads went through the open window, it was like a door to another dimension had opened. It was as if we were looking into another world.

In the distance, I could see blue and white striped carnival tents, and lots of really cool rides. There were people everywhere. Children and adults, carnival workers. Some of them weren't very far away.

And the *music*.

The calliope music was crisp and clear, no longer distant and wispy. The happy sound rose into a perfectly blue, cloudless sky.

In the distance I saw a juggler tossing balls into the air, expertly catching each one and throwing them back up, high into the sky.

Scott gasped. I drew in a breath and held it. Courtney spoke.

"Okay," she said quietly. *"I know you guys are playing a joke. But . . . how are you doing this?"*

"This is no joke, Courtney," I said. *"This is no joke at all."*

I was terrified . . . and I think Courtney and Scott were, too.

But we were also mesmerized. What we were seeing couldn't be real . . . and yet it was. I *knew* what I was seeing. I knew what I was *hearing.*

Suddenly, a figure emerged right in front of us. It was as if he came out of nowhere. We all jumped out of sheer surprise.

It was a boy.

He was wearing black pants and black shoes, and a white shirt. His hair was black and cut very short.

And he was looking right at us.

"Hi!" he said. He bowed, then stood up straight and spread his arms. "Welcome to the carnival!"

The three of us said nothing. I, for one, was too shocked to speak. I think Scott and Courtney were, too.

"Yes, sir-ree!" the boy bellowed. "This is the carnival that everyone wants to come to! So many things to see! So many things to do! You will enjoy yourselves like you've never enjoyed yourselves before! Like you never will again!"

The three of us still said nothing. I think we were too freaked out to respond.

"Oh, come on!" the boy said, spreading his arms wide. "It's fun here! There is so much more to see and do!"

I knew that what we were seeing just couldn't be real . . . but it was. I was seeing it with my very own eyes.

"Well, it looks like a lot of fun," I said to the boy. "But it's getting late. We have to go home."

The boy shook his head. "All time stops here. You can spend as much time as you want in the carnival . . . but in your world, no time will have passed at all."

I looked around. It sure looked like it would be fun.

But something wasn't right. I knew it.

"Maybe some other time," Scott said.

"Well, you guys can go home," Courtney said. "But I'm going to check this place out!"

Before I could stop her, Courtney had climbed through the window . . . *and into the carnival!*

10

"Courtney!" I shouted. *"What are you doing?!?!"*

"Oh, don't be such a chicken," she said. She was now standing in front of us. She *should* have been standing inside a room in the house . . . but the room didn't exist.

A carnival did.

An honest-to-goodness carnival, right before my very eyes.

"It's really fun," the boy urged. He waved to us, then she pointed at Courtney. "See? She's okay. Come on in!"

Courtney was looking around at the carnival. "This is just incredible!" she said. "It's like another world here! Come on, you guys!"

Courtney began to walk toward the carnival midway.

"Courtney! Don't go!" I shouted.

"I'll be right back!" she replied with a quick turn of her head. "I just want to take a look around."

"Don't worry," the boy said with a wave. "She'll be fine. She'll have fun."

And then he skipped off, joining the crowd of people in the midway. In the distance, Courtney was walking slowly, milling through the throngs of people. She turned, looked at us, and waved. Then she disappeared behind an enormous tent.

"Want to check it out?" Scott asked.

"I do," I said, "but this is too freaky. A Carnival? Inside a *house?* I mean . . . it's impossible!"

"But here it is," Scott said. "You're seeing the same thing I'm seeing."

"Let's wait for Courtney to come back," I said.

As we waited, I backed away from the window.

The carnival vanished. I could see Scott leaning on the window sill, but he appeared to be leaning into darkness. The calliope music played on, but it was faint.

I leaned forward again, placing my elbows on the edge of the window. As soon as my face was inside, the strange carnival appeared again, and the music became clearer.

The minutes ticked by, and there still was no sign of Courtney.

"Where did she go?" I wondered aloud.

"I haven't seen her since she went behind that tent," Scott said. "Do you think we should go find her?"

"I don't know," I replied. "But I'm getting worried."

Suddenly, a scream pierced the air, cutting through the noise of the carnival. It was shrill and long. I recognized it instantly.

It was Courtney . . . and I could tell right away that she wasn't joking this time!

11

We knew what we had to do.

Without saying a word, Scott and I leapt through the window at the same time and began running toward the carnival midway.

"Where did that scream come from?" Scott asked as our feet pounded the hard-packed dirt.

"I think she's over there!" I exclaimed, pointing toward a large Ferris wheel.

We darted through the crowd, weaving in and around people. When we reached the other side of the Ferris wheel, we stopped.

Before us was a roller coaster. It was an old one. Its steel tracks snaked high into the air, winding around in wiry loops and twisting corkscrews.

"Look!" Scott said, pointing. "It's Courtney!"

The roller coaster cars were nearing the end of the ride, slowing as they approached. Courtney was waving to us, and she had a wide smile on her face.

I was relieved. Courtney was fine, after all. She'd screamed in excitement while she was on the roller coaster.

When the cars stopped, she unbuckled her safety harness and climbed out, and rushed over to where we were.

"This is awesome!" she exclaimed. "Everything is free! All of the rides . . . even the food! It's all free!"

There was a girl standing in line, waiting to board the roller coaster. She wore a pink dress, with matching pink ribbons in her hair.

"Of course everything is free," she said. "Everything is free at *this* carnival." Then she turned away.

Scott looked at the watch on his wrist. Then he tapped it with his fingers.

"Look at this," he said curiously. He held out his arm for us to see. "Look at my watch."

I looked at the round dial on his wrist, and so did Courtney.

"It stopped!" I exclaimed.

"Do you think that time has really stopped while we're here?" Courtney asked.

"I don't know," Scott replied. "But if time has stopped, and everything's free . . . this is like a dream come true!"

"But how can this be?" I said. "This isn't real. It can't be."

"I don't care if it's real or not," Scott replied. "Let's hang out and have some fun. When we get tired, we'll go back . . . and no time will have gone by! We could stay here for hours, and our parents won't even miss us because time has stopped!"

"If time has stopped, how will we be able to tell when a few hours is up?" I asked smartly. "I mean . . . we've been standing here talking for two minutes, at least. Time must be passing, somehow."

"So what?" Courtney said. "I'm with Scott. I say we hang out for a while before we go home."

And that's what we did. We rode the rides, we played games. We ate hot dogs and elephant ears and cotton candy. After a while, my uneasiness went away. The carnival was really kind of cool, and I was already making plans to come back.

A few hours *did* go by. Scott's watch had stopped, but I knew that we'd been at the carnival for a long time. I was ready to go home and go to bed.

"Let's call it a day," I said to Courtney as we strode down the midway. "I'm tired."

"Yeah, me too," she said.

"I can't wait to come back here," Scott exclaimed, throwing his arms up into the air. "Think about it! On a rainy day, we can come here! The sun is shining, the weather is perfect—"

"—and everything is free!" Courtney finished. "I almost don't want to go home."

Just then, a little girl turned and looked at us. She must have been about five years old, and she had short, brown hair and chubby cheeks. She was holding the hand of an older boy, and I presumed that he was her brother.

And she had a curious look on her face.

"But . . . you *can't* go home," the little girl said.

"Huh?" replied Courtney.

"You can't go home," the little girl repeated. *"Everyone knows that. Nobody can leave the carnival. This is your home now."*

12

I shuddered.

"What do you mean?" I asked the little girl.

"Home," she said. "This *is* home. It's home for all of us. You, too."

An awful chill began at the top of my head and swept through my entire body. I looked at Courtney and Scott. I could tell that they, too, had the same horrified feeling.

The little girl moved away, towed gently by her brother.

"She's only kidding," Courtney said with a nervous laugh. "Come on."

I wasn't all that convinced. I knew I'd feel a whole lot better once we were safely at home.

We walked through the midway and back in the direction of the window—but what we saw was more than just a window.

It was a house.

The Madhouse.

It looked just like it did at the end of the street, except now it was surrounded by rides and tents and carnival events. There were people all around, but no one was near the house.

"How can that be?" I asked. "When we came through the window, we entered from the *outside* of the house. Now it looks like we're still outside of it."

"Maybe it's a different house," Scott said.

But the closer we got, the more certain I was that it indeed *was* the same house.

"Look!" Courtney exclaimed. She raised her arm and pointed. "It has the same porch. And the same windows as before. It *is* the same house!"

Suddenly, a boy walked up to us. It was the same boy that had invited us into the carnival.

"Pretty fun, huh?" he asked.

"How do we get home?" Scott replied.

The boy smiled. "Why . . . you *are* home," he said. "This *is* home."

I shook my head. "No, it's not," I said. "It might be *your* home, but it's not *our* home."

"The carnival is everyone's home," the boy replied. "Besides . . . why would you want to leave?"

"Because we want to go home," Scott answered. He pointed toward the old house that loomed before us. "Can't we just climb through the window?"

The boy's smile faded, and a strange look came over his face. He shook his head slowly.

"Jeffrey won't let anyone leave," he said.

"Who's Jeffrey?" I asked.

"Jeffrey is why we're here. Jeffrey won't let anyone leave. Jeffrey never lets anyone leave the carnival once they're here."

"It looks like the same house we came through," Courtney replied. She pointed. "I can see the very same window right there."

Again, the boy shook his head. "You can't," he said.

"But that's where we came from," I insisted.

"Oh, you can come *through* from the other side," he explained, "but you can't go *back* through. Lots of people have tried."

"You . . . you mean there are other people who have come through besides us?" I asked.

"Sure," the boy replied. "That's how everyone got here. All time has stopped, and most people don't know how long they've been here. Actually, it's pretty cool. You'll learn to like it."

"But who is Jeffrey?" I asked again. "And why won't he let anyone leave?"

The boy frowned. "Jeffrey is the one who created all of this," he said, spreading his arms wide. "He's a very powerful wizard. He made everything you see here."

"A wizard?!?!" I exclaimed.

The boy nodded his head.

"But why won't he let anyone leave?" Scott asked.

The boy shrugged. "Beats me," he said. "Besides . . . who would want to? Everything you could ever want is right here."

"Well, we want to go home," Courtney said. "Can Jeffrey give us that?"

"Well, I suppose you could go and ask him," the boy replied. "But no one has ever done that."

"Why?" I asked.

"It's too dangerous. Jeffrey lives far away."

"I don't care," I said. "I want to go and talk to him. He has no right to make us . . . or anyone else . . . stay here!"

"Well, like I said," the boy continued, "you can go ask him. But it's not a very easy thing to do."

"Why?" Scott asked.

The boy pointed toward the old house. "Because Jeffrey lives in there. In the house."

"Well, then, that's easy," Courtney said. "We''ll just go in the house and tell him that he has to let us go home, or my dad is going to come over here and then he'll *really* be in trouble!"

"Well, the first step is to get into the house," the boy said. "There are many different realms inside. Then we'll find out where to go from there."

"Do you know how to get to his house?" I asked.

"I think so," the boy replied. "I found his house a long time ago. And I could probably find it again."

It sounded simple enough . . . but it wasn't going to be. We were about to begin one of the most terrifying journeys of our lives.

13

The four of us began walking toward the house.

"What's your name?" I asked the boy. It occurred to me that we hadn't introduced ourselves.

He looked at me a moment, then he looked at Courtney and Scott. "I'm Tony," he said.

"I'm Amber, and this is Courtney and Scott."

"Nice to meet you," he said.

"It'll be nicer if we can get out of here and go home," Courtney said.

We reached the house. For sure, it looked just like the house we had entered before.

Too weird.

"We're going to have to be careful," Tony said as he stepped up onto the porch. "I have no idea where we'll end up."

"What do you mean?" Scott asked.

"I mean just that. When we go inside the house, we might find ourselves in a jungle surrounded by tigers. Or maybe we'll wind up in a desert. Who knows?"

"That's crazy!" I exclaimed.

"It might be, but that's what happens. That's why no one can leave. Once you enter the house, it's almost impossible to find your way out."

"Wait a minute," Courtney said. "I thought you said we were going to find this 'Jeffrey' kid. Now you're saying that we might get lost. Which is it?"

"Both," Tony replied. "Finding Jeffrey is pretty difficult, because he travels all over. That's why no one here at the carnival wants to go and look for him. I think we can find his house, though."

"So, when we walk though that door, we aren't really going into a house?" I asked.

"Yes and no," Tony answered. "We're inside the house . . . but each time we walk through a door, we'll travel to a different realm. Kind of like the way you came to the carnival from your world."

"Well, let's get this over with," Courtney said. "I want to go home."

We followed Tony up the porch. He stopped by the door.

"Ready?" he said.

The three of us nodded, and Tony grasped the door handle.

"Here we go," he said, and he gave the door a push. It swung open, and Tony let go of the knob.

And on the other side of the door—

A room.

That's all.

It looked just like an old house with no furniture. The walls were bare, and the floors were made of wood.

"But I thought you said—"

"Hang on a minute," Tony interrupted. "Watch."

And with that, he took a step forward, through the door . . . and disappeared!

"Whoa!" Scott exclaimed. "Where did he go?"

"He must have traveled to another realm!" I said.

"What are we waiting for?" Courtney said. "Let's get moving!"

She grabbed my hand, and I grabbed Scott's hand.

"Ready?" Courtney asked.

"Ready," Scott and I said at the same time.

"On three," Courtney began. "One, two . . ."

I hope we're doing the right thing, I thought.

"Three!"

The three of us stepped through the doorway—and into a world that I could have never possibly imagined.

14

The moment we stepped through that door, everything changed. The world as we knew it had been left behind.

Now we were standing in an enormous forest. Trees towered thousands of feet into the air, and their trunks were bigger than houses. I remember seeing pictures of California redwood trees that were big enough to drive a car through. Well, let me tell you . . . the trees that we were seeing now were ten times bigger than that.

And Tony was there, too. He was right in front of us.

"Cool, huh?" he said.

But the three of us were too stunned to say anything.

"Jeffrey created all of this," Tony continued. "He's a very powerful wizard."

"This is unbelievable," Scott said softly. "I've never seen trees that big."

Just then, I noticed a leaf falling. At first, it was really high in the sky. As is gently fell to earth, it got bigger and bigger and bigger.

Then I realized something.

The leaf was as big as a truck . . . and it was going to come down right on top of us!

Tony noticed it, too. "Everybody scatter!" he ordered, and the four of us dashed off in different directions.

Sure enough, the leaf landed right where we had been standing. I don't know if it would have hurt us or not, but it sure was better to be safe than sorry.

We gathered around the large leaf. It was green, and the edges curled up, resembling somewhat of a boat. In fact, the more I looked at it, the more I realized that it looked a *lot* like a boat. An oak leaf boat.

"So, where do we go now?" Courtney asked.

"First," Tony said, "let's have a look around. Maybe we can see Jeffrey's house. If not, then we'll have to start hiking."

"I thought you said you've been to his house before," Courtney said.

"I have," Tony replied. "But I can't remember which doors I went through. Don't worry, though. We'll find his house."

The four of us stuck together, wandering around the huge trees. In Missouri we have big trees . . . but none that would even come close to the trees that I was seeing now!

"Maybe we'll come to a door soon," Tony said.

"A door?" I replied.

Tony nodded. "It'll look just like a door to a house. However, there won't be any walls around it. It will just be a door. That will be one of the doors within the house. It will lead to yet another realm."

This was all very confusing—but we had no other choice. If we wanted to go home, we would have to find Jeffrey.

We wandered about for a few minutes, but we didn't see anything that looked like a house. Matter of fact, we didn't see much of anything at all, except gigantic trees.

"Well, let's head off this way," Tony said. "Sooner or later, we'll have to either come to a door or find Jeffrey's house."

And so we followed Tony. We asked him all kinds of questions while we walked. We asked him how Jeffrey had become a wizard and how old he was. Tony said that Jeffrey had always been a wizard, and that he looked like any other kid our age . . .with one exception.

Tony told us that Jeffrey is hundreds of years old!

"Yeah, right," Courtney sneered.

"It's true," Tony said. "He really is. When we find him, you can ask him."

"Well, I hope we find him pretty quick," griped Courtney. "I'm not too crazy about traveling through different realms and stuff. As a matter of fact—"

"*Shhhh!*" Tony hissed, raising a finger to his lips. We stopped walking and listened.

"What is it?" I whispered.

"Probably nothing," Tony replied. "I just thought I heard something."

"Like . . .what kinds of animals are around here?" Scott asked.

"It's not the animals that we have to worry about," Tony answered.

"Well, what, then?" I asked.

But Tony didn't need to answer. When I saw what had been hiding behind the tree, I gasped — then I screamed.

And Tony was right. We didn't have to worry about animals.

We had to worry about the terrible monster that was now coming right for us!

I couldn't believe my eyes. Not far away was an enormous, six-legged creature. It was the biggest living creature I had ever seen before. Twice as big as an elephant, even.

Courtney screamed. "What is that?!?!" Scott gasped.

"That," Tony replied, "is nothing but an ordinary ant."

"Ordinary?!?!" I replied. "He's . . .he's as big as a house!"

"That's not true," Tony replied. "It's not the ant that is different. It's us."

"Huh?" asked Courtney.

"It's not the ant that's big," he answered. "It's just that we're small. I've been here before. When we entered into this realm, we shrunk."

We ducked behind one of the enormous trees and peered around the side, keeping our eyes on the huge ant.

"Do you think he'll hurt us?" I asked.

"Only if he sees us," Tony replied.

That *wasn't* what I wanted to hear.

"Don't worry," Tony continued. "I've been here before. I don't think he'll bother us. He's busy looking for food."

"I hope he doesn't think that four kids would make a nice meal," Courtney said.

"Or dessert," I added.

I was really scared, but, I have to admit, the ant was pretty cool looking. I could see him really well. I'd never seen an ant in such detail. I could see his long antennae, and how they flicked about like snakes. The ant's color was a dark brown-black, and his skeleton was shiny. I read somewhere that, unlike us humans, ants have a skeleton on the outside of their bodies. So what we were looking at wasn't the ant's skin, but his actual skeleton.

Suddenly, the ant turned and began coming toward us.

"Okay guys," Tony said quietly. "Time to move. He's getting too close."

The four of us ducked behind the tree and began to slink away as quietly as we could. We slunk around gigantic tree trunks and huge blades of grass. As I looked at our surroundings, I began to realize that, no matter how crazy it seemed, Tony was right. We had shrunk.

I glanced over my shoulder. The ant was farther away, but he was still coming toward us. We would have to change direction if we were going to keep away from him.

Before I could turn my head back around, I came to an abrupt halt. Courtney had stopped ahead of me, and I ran into her. Ahead of her, Scott had stopped, and so had Tony.

"What is it?" I asked.

Tony pointed, but I couldn't see anything.

We waited, and suddenly, we saw what Tony had been pointing at.

On the tree in front of us, another ant was crawling. He was coming down the tree!

"Don't anybody move," Tony said. *"Not a single muscle."*

I don't think I could have moved if I tried!

We watched as the ant climbed down the tree. He was only a few feet in front of us, but I don't think he had any idea we were there.

And I must say, I sure was relieved when the giant ant reached the ground and began walking the other way.

But not for long.

In the next moment, the enormous insect stopped. His antennae flickered back and forth.

He turned around, and there was no mistake.

We'd been spotted.

Not only had we been spotted, but the ant began to crawl toward us . . .and fast!

16

Nobody had to say a thing. It was like we all sensed at the exact same time that it was time to run.

And that's what we did.

We turned and began to run as fast as we could, darting around giant blades of grass and bounding over small sticks. We didn't look to see if the ant was behind us. We knew he was there, and besides . . . we couldn't risk tripping and falling.

But I had no idea where we would run. Tony seemed to know where he was going, so the only thing we could do was follow him . . .and hope that we could run faster than the ant!

Finally, I couldn't stand it anymore. I had to know where the ant was. I turned my head, expecting to see the huge beast right behind me.

Thankfully, we had put some distance between us. The ant was still coming, but he looked more curious than anything.

But all too soon, our luck ran out. I heard Scott gasp, and then Courtney. We had run right to the edge of a cliff. I could see for what seemed liked miles. Far below was a valley, and I could see what appeared to be a river snaking through a thick forest.

"We're trapped!" Courtney shouted. "There's nowhere to go!"

Oh, how I wish that we were still back at the carnival! Even better, I wished we were back home. I wished I'd never *heard* of the Missouri Madhouse!

The ant kept coming closer. We had to think fast.

"Can we climb down onto a ledge?" Scott asked.

Tony shook his head. "There isn't any ledge," he said.

"The ant is getting closer!" Courtney exclaimed.

But there was nowhere to run.

I began looking around on the ground for a small stick or twig that I could pick up and use to defend myself. I knew that it probably wouldn't help much, but it was the only thing I could think of. But there weren't any sticks nearby. The only thing close was a giant leaf, like the one we had watched fall from the tree. It's edges were curled up, and it looked like a giant bowl.

And *that* gave me an idea.

"Guys! Let's get on the ground and pull this leaf over us! We can hide under the leaf!"

Tony snapped his fingers, and his eyes lit up. "Even better . . . climb inside!"

"What?!?!" Courtney exclaimed.

"Climb inside! I have an idea!"

We scrambled into the leaf. All the while, the ant kept coming. In seconds, he would be upon us.

But Tony did an odd thing. He put one leg in the leaf, and began pushing the ground with the other. The leaf started to move, but he was pushing us closer and closer to the edge of the cliff!

"Stop!" I shrieked. "You're going to push us over the edge!"

But Tony didn't pay any attention. The ant was only a few feet away, and I could see its giant pinchers beginning to open and close.

"Tony, what are you—"

Suddenly, the leaf began to slide. Tony pulled his foot in and tumbled into the leaf, just seconds before the ant would have snatched him up.

The leaf slid slowly . . . and suddenly plummeted over the edge of the cliff.

We were falling!

17

Courtney screamed, and her hand flew to her mouth. Then suddenly, she stopped screaming.

We were falling, all right . . . but we were safely inside the leaf, and we seemed to be gently floating down. It was like we were in a small canoe or boat. The leaf rocked and spun gently. High above, the ant had reached the cliff and was looking down. Then he disappeared from sight.

"That was close," Tony said.

"Good thinking!" Scott exclaimed. "I thought that all four of us were goners!"

"It feels like we're flying," I said.

"We're not really flying," Tony corrected. "We don't have any control of the leaf. Hopefully, we'll land right on the ground without any problem."

Below us, the valley was getting closer and closer. I was really nervous. I've flown in an airplane before, but this was nothing like that at all. This was more like riding on a bumpy elevator.

"But what are we going to do when we land?" Courtney asked.

"We should come to a door pretty soon," Tony replied. "Then we'll be able to enter another realm."

"I thought we were looking for Jeffrey," I said.

"We are," Tony replied. "But I don't think he's here. We'll have to search each room. Each door leads to another room, to another realm. We're in a big house . . . a big house of different realms. Don't worry . . . we'll find him."

Weird, weird, weird.

Our leaf continued to fall, tipping and bobbing, whirling and swirling. I was getting dizzy, and I hoped that we'd reach the ground soon.

But that wasn't going to happen.

All too soon we realized that the leaf wasn't going to land on the ground. It was going to land in the river.

Which wouldn't have been a problem, except for what was *in* the water.

"What are all of those things moving in the river?" I asked.

"I don't think you want to know," Tony replied.

Suddenly, I *knew* what was in the water. My stomach dropped to my feet. There was no way the four of us would make it out of the river alive.

Just beneath the surface of the water were huge creatures that I instantly recognized.

The river was filled —

With sharks!

18

We screamed in unison:

"*SHARKS!*"

It was unbelievable. I mean . . . who ever heard of a shark in Missouri?!?! I thought sharks only lived in the ocean.

Not so.

"There's got to be fifty of them, right below us!" I gasped.

"If we land in the water, we're going to be gobbled up!" shrieked Courtney.

"We've got to try and steer the leaf so we don't land in the water!" Tony said. "Everyone! Over to my side of the leaf! Hurry!"

We did as he said, but I didn't know how that would steer the leaf. There certainly weren't any controls or anything. We didn't even have anything to hold on to.

But as soon as we were all on the same side, the leaf began to tilt.

"Lean over the edge!" Tony ordered. "We've got to make this side of the leaf tilt down so the wind will push the other side!"

Below us, in the river, I could see the sharks schooling around. It looked like they were waiting for us.

"That's it!" Tony cried. "It's working!"

Our leaf was almost sideways now, and it felt like we were in a canoe that was tipping over. In fact, if we leaned any more over the edge, I was sure that we would fall right out!

But Tony was right. I could feel our course changing. The leaf wasn't dropping straight down anymore, but, rather, drifting to the side. The wind was pushing the side of the leaf, and we were drifting away from the river.

Regardless, it was still going to be close, and if the leaf landed in the water, no matter how close to shore we would be, I knew that the sharks would get us. There were still below, swimming in circles, waiting.

Like they were waiting for lunch.

The wind rushed past, roaring in our ears as we floated down.

"Are we going to make it?" Courtney shouted above the roaring wind.

"I think we are!" Tony shouted. "But it's going to be close!"

Down, down, down we went, the wind rushing past. The leaf bobbled and wobbled a bit, and once I thought I was going to fall out.

"We're going to make it!" Scott suddenly shouted.

He was right! Below us was dry land! The wind had pushed our giant leaf far enough over, and we would land on the shore, after all.

"Hang on!" Tony said. "It's going to be a bumpy landing!"

The ground approached faster and faster, until all of a sudden—

Crunch!

"Oof!" I grunted as we hit the ground.

"Ouch!" Courtney said.

We toppled out of the leaf and rolled to the ground. I jumped to my feet instantly, just in case one of those nasty sharks decided to jump out of the water and attack. Courtney, Scott, and Tony didn't waste any time getting up, either.

"That was close," Courtney said.

"Too close," I agreed.

I turned and looked at the river. I could see shark fins everywhere. On the other side of the river, giant trees loomed tall and forbidding. Behind us, a huge rock wall stretched high into the sky. It was hard to believe that we just floated down in a leaf!

"Just what kind of place is this?" Scott asked.

"I told you," Tony said. "All of this stuff was created by Jeffrey."

"I wish I could make different realms and stuff," Scott said.

"Come on," Tony said, pointing. "That door should be over there somewhere."

"Just what else should we be on the lookout for?" Courtney asked. "I mean . . . are we going to be attacked by a giant earthworm or something?"

Tony laughed. "Don't worry. I think our troubles are over now."

But when we heard a loud screeching sound from the sky above us, we knew that our troubles had just begun.

19

We turned and looked up just as a dark shadow passed over us.

It was a bird of some sort! Not just a bird, but a super-huge giant one . . . bigger than a jet plane!

"Run!" Tony shrieked. He bolted, the rest of us following hard on his heels.

The giant bird screeched again and swooped down, so close that I could feel the air from its huge, flapping wings.

"Don't let him get you!" Tony screamed as we bounded across the hard-packed ground.

I heard another screech and the bird swooped down again, coming even closer this time. I zigzagged as I ran, hoping to stay out of reach of its razor sharp talons.

"That thing is going to eat us!" Courtney cried. "There's no way we can get away from him!"

"Yes we can!" Tony exclaimed. He pointed as he ran. "There's the door, right up there!"

Just ahead of us, on the ground, was the door he spoke of. No house, no walls or windows—just a door. A single, wooden door with a brass knob.

I heard another screech from above, and once again the dark shadow of the bird swooped down over us. I pumped my legs as hard as I could, again, zig-zagging back and forth. The wind created from the flapping of the monstrous bird's wings was strong enough to nearly blow us over.

"Almost there!" Tony shouted.

I made a quick move to the left as I ran, and it was a good thing—because at that very moment, the bird snapped out one of his claws and tried to grab me! If I hadn't zigzagged at that very moment, I would've been a goner!

Suddenly, Tony reached the door. In a split-second, he grasped the brass knob and turned. The door opened up, and he disappeared through the opening. Courtney followed, then Scott.

I took two more huge leaps, closed my eyes and dove headfirst through the open door. I heard it slam behind me, as I tumbled to the ground. I hit something soft and I heard Courtney cry out, and I realized that I had probably landed on her.

I opened my eyes, and gasped at what I saw.

20

We were in a hallway. Not just any hallway, mind you . . . but a *stone* hallway!

The floor beneath our feet, the walls—even the ceiling—were made out of flat, dark gray stones. The air smelled damp and musty, like an old basement. A torch burned on the wall, casting a smoky, yellow light.

I rolled to my side and sat up. Courtney got to her feet. Tony and Scott remained on the floor.

"All right," Courtney said quietly as she brushed herself off. "I'm afraid to ask . . . but where are we?"

"It looks like we're in some kind of castle," Tony replied.

"This just gets creepier and creepier," I said, getting to my feet. I walked over to a wall and touched a stone. It was cool and smooth.

"Well, wherever we are," Scott said, "there's only one way we can go."

Scott was right. Behind us was the wood door. It was closed, and I wasn't going to open it, that's for sure. There was no way I wanted to go back to that realm and get eaten by some giant bird!

"Let's go see where this leads," Tony said. He leapt to his feet.

"All of this because you had to go and play in that silly carnival," Scott said to Courtney.

"Hey, don't blame me," Courtney snapped. "You rode the rides, too. You had fun. This is just as much your fault as it is mine."

"Don't worry, you guys," Tony said. "I'm telling you . . . we'll get out of here, as soon as we find Jeffrey. You have to admit . . . this is kind of fun, isn't it?"

"Yes and no," I said. "I like exploring different places, but I don't want to be chased by giant creatures."

"Me neither," Courtney agreed. "I'd rather be home in Blue Springs."

We walked down the dimly lit stone hallway. There were no windows, no paintings; nothing on the walls at all, except for the torches that were spaced about twenty feet apart.

"Hey, look up ahead!" Scott said suddenly. I squinted in the murky light to see what he was talking about.

It was a room! The hallway opened into a room!

We walked faster, and then stopped when the hallway suddenly ended. There was a tall, arch-shaped doorway in front of us. We walked under the arch and into a very large room. A solid gold chandelier hung from the ceiling, with several dozen candles emitting a soft, wavering light. Torches lined the walls of the room, casting a smoky, yellow light, just as they had in the hallway. On the far wall a fire burned in an enormous fireplace. In the center of the room was a large table with several chairs around it. On our right was a stone staircase that wound upwards along the wall, and disappeared into the darkness above.

On the walls, between the torches, were portraits of people. They appeared to be very old. The men in them wore capes; the women, flowing white dresses.

"We *are* in some sort of castle," I whispered.

No one said anything more for a few minutes. We just stared at the pictures on the walls and at the fire in the fireplace.

"This is terrific," Courtney said glumly. "We get attacked by a giant ant, almost get eaten by sharks, a giant bird chases us, and now we're lost in a castle. What's going to happen next?"

"Well, there has to be a way out of here," Tony said. "Somewhere."

"Maybe we're in Jeffrey's house," Scott said.

Tony shook his head. "No, this isn't Jeffrey's house. I'm sure of it."

"Maybe we can find whoever lives here, and they can tell us," I offered.

"Hello?" Courtney called out. Her voice echoed through the large room. "Anybody home?"

There was no answer. We heard no sounds at all except for the crackle of the fire and the sputters and snaps from the burning torches on the walls.

"Up there," Tony said. "Let's see where that staircase goes." He reached over and took a torch from the wall. "Now we'll be able to see better. Come on."

We started up the stone stairs. It was a good thing that Tony had grabbed that torch, too, because the further up the staircase we climbed the darker it became. There were no torches along the wall of the stairs.

"I feel like Tom Sawyer exploring a cave," Scott said.

"Tom who?" Tony asked.

"Tom Sawyer was a character created more than a hundred years ago by an author named Mark Twain, who lived in Missouri," replied Scott.

"Tom Sawyer never rode in a leaf or got attacked by a big bird," Courtney said.

"Yeah, but this is kind of cool, don't you think?"

Scott was right. It was kind of fun, exploring an old castle . . . now that we were out of danger.

Problem was, danger was on its way . . . and we were about to find it.

21

At the top of the stairs there was a long, dark, stone corridor. There were no torches except the one that Tony carried, so it was difficult to know just how far the hallway went.

"Come on," Tony said quietly, and he started out. We followed without a word, and the only sound was that of our footsteps echoing down the hall.

We hadn't gone very far when we came to an open door. Tony stopped and swung the torch in front of the doorway, and the flames illuminated a small, empty room.

"There's nothing in there," Courtney said.

"Let's keep going," Scott said, and we started off again. Soon, we came to another empty room, and then another.

"There's the end of the hall, up ahead," I said.

"And there's a door," Tony said.

"Is it a door to another realm?" Scott asked.

Tony shook his head. "No, I'm afraid not. I'm not sure what's beyond it. Probably just another empty room, though."

The door had a large, iron doorknob. Tony reached out and grasped it.

"It's unlocked," he whispered.

"Open it!" I whispered back.

Slowly, Tony turned the knob. There was a series of heavy clicks and clunks, and Tony pushed.

The door opened! It made no sound, no squeaks or squeals—but in the glow of the torch light, we could see that the room was empty . . . or, so we first thought.

Because at the far wall, on top of a large table, was a long, oblong box.

"A . . . A . . . Amber," Courtney stammered. "Is . . . is that what I think it is?"

"I don't know," I whispered back. "What do you think it is?"

But Courtney didn't reply. She didn't need to. We all knew what was on the table.

It was a coffin.

"Whoa," Scott whispered.

"Double whoa," I said.

Tony leaned closer and held the torch high. Then he took a couple of steps closer. I followed, staying one step behind him and looking over his shoulder.

It was a coffin, all right. It was all black, except for gold trim around the edges. There was some strange writing engraved on it, but it was a language that I'd never seen before. In the wavering glow of the torch, it looked spooky.

"Let's open it!" Scott whispered from behind me.

"Let's not, and say we did," I said. "I'm not opening that thing!"

"Yeah, let's!" Courtney said. "Let's see what's inside! That would be kew-*wool!*"

Scott brushed past me and approached the coffin, inspecting the side of it.

"There has to be something on this thing to grab onto so we can pop the lid open," he said.

Courtney joined Scott, and Tony held the light high.

"Here it is!" Courtney suddenly exclaimed. "There is a handle right here."

"And here's one, here!" Scott said. "Come on, Amber . . . give us a hand!"

Reluctantly, I took a place between Scott and Courtney.

"On the count of three," Scott said, "we'll lift. One . . . two . . . *three!*"

It was a struggle, but the coffin lid slowly began to raise. Scott grunted, and Courtney gritted her teeth. I had a difficult time, too. The lid weighed a ton.

Finally, we were able to lift it all the way up — and when we stepped back to let the light from the torch illuminate the inside of the coffin, we knew we had made a *huge* mistake.

Inside the coffin . . . was a vampire!

22

All four of us took a giant step backward. As we did, the light from our torch receded from his face, making him look even creepier.

And how did I know he was a vampire?

Well, he looked like every single vampire I had ever seen on television. His face was bone-white, and his lips were bright red. A triangular patch of hair receded a tiny bit down his forehead. His eyes were closed, and his arms crossed his chest. He was wearing what appeared to be a black suit and a black cloak; in the flickering light I couldn't be sure.

I don't know how long we stood there, staring, our terror simmering like water on a stove. The torch popped and cracked, and the dancing flames caused the coffin to appear to rock back and forth.

Finally, I spoke.

"I . . . I think he's sleeping," I whispered quietly.

"Then let's let him sleep," Courtney said. Her voice trembled, and I could tell she was just as scared as I was.

"Good idea," Tony said, and he took another step back. Scott, Courtney and I followed, and soon we were back in the hall.

"I didn't think vampires were real," Courtney said.

"Me neither," I replied, shaking my head. "He sure gave me the creeps."

"We have to get out of here," Scott said. "We have to find the door that leads to another realm."

"Let's go back to that main room," Tony suggested. "At least it's not as dark there."

We began walking, relieved that we hadn't disturbed the vampire. Man! I had never been so scared in my life!

As we walked down the stone hall, we again passed the empty rooms. Suddenly, a dark shadow burst from one of the rooms! We froze in our tracks.

It was the vampire! He was right in front of us!

"Going somewhere, children? Hmmm? I don't think so. I think you'll be staying for a little while. . . ."

Gulp!

23

We were in a lot of trouble.

I'd heard about everything that vampires can do. They can change into bats and fly off into the night. They can make themselves invisible and walk through walls.

But vampires aren't *real*. I mean . . . they're not supposed to be, anyway.

All of a sudden, Tony leapt forward, waving the torch. The vampire jumped back and shrank away from the flames.

"Run!" Tony shrieked, and we sprang up and away like cheetahs. Tony was in the lead, carrying the torch, and I was right behind him. Scott and Courtney were right behind me.

When we came to the stairs, we kept going, bounding two at a time. I wanted out of the castle, and I couldn't run fast enough.

At the bottom of the staircase we stopped. We were all panting, out of breath, and gasping for air.

"Where . . . where now?" I huffed between breaths.

"I . . . I guess we'll have . . . have to go . . . go back the way . . . way we came," Tony panted. "Come on!"

We were all still out of breath, but we knew we had to keep going. We wanted to get away from that freaky vampire as soon as we possibly could.

We hurried down the hall, backtracking our way to the door where we'd passed through. I didn't know if that giant bird would be hanging around, but I didn't care. I'd take my chances with a giant bird over a vampire any day!

"There it is, right up ahead," Tony said.

I was relieved, but still fearful, halfway expecting the vampire to suddenly appear in front of us.

Tony reached the door first and grasped the handle.

"Wait," Courtney said. "Open it just a little bit and poke your head through. Just in case that bird is waiting for us."

"Good idea," Tony replied.

But he never got the chance to open the door. Instead, the door opened . . . all by itself.

And on the other side?

You guessed it.

The vampire.

He took a step through the door and into a hallway. The door slammed shut behind him.

"Now children," he hissed, "you're not being very polite. Won't you stay . . . for a *bite?*"

When we heard those words, we did the only thing we could do:

Scream.

24

There was nowhere to run. I guess we could have ran back to the main hall, but the vampire seemed to have a way of getting there before us.

"Really, now," the vampire said. "Won't you *please* stay for a bite?"

"Please, Mr. Vampire, sir," Scott said, taking a step back. "We don't want you to bite us. We just want to go home."

A strange look came over the vampire's face. "Bite you?" he said. "Who said anything about *biting* you?"

"Well, that's what vampires, do, isn't it?" Courtney asked. "Don't they bite people in the neck?"

The vampire suddenly burst into laughter. "That's ridiculous!" he exclaimed, and he laughed some more. "My friends, I merely meant that it is not often that I receive guests. I'd like you to join me at my table for dinner."

Things were getting weirder all the time.

"You mean . . . like . . . have a bite to eat?" I asked.

"Precisely," the vampire said. "I am Count Dracula. Please be my guests for dinner."

Count Dracula?!?!?

"Hey, you're famous!" Courtney said. "Someone wrote a book about you! Can I have your autograph?"

"Certainly, certainly," Count Dracula replied. "Come! Let's have a meal before you leave. You must be hungry. Children are always hungry." He brushed past us and began gliding down the hall. The rest of us didn't move.

Count Dracula turned. "Well? Aren't you coming?"

I shrugged; Courtney frowned. Then the four of us followed the vampire down the hall and back to the huge room.

"Ah! Splendid!" we heard the Count say as he entered the large room.

And when the four of us approached the main hall, we stopped short with a gasp. None of us could believe what we were seeing.

The table in the large room was filled . . . with food! Moments ago, when we ran past, it was empty . . . but now it was set with all kinds of delicious food!

"How . . . how did *that* get there?" I whispered to Courtney.

"You got me," she replied quietly.

"Please," Count Dracula said as he stepped toward the table. "Sit! Be my guests, and we will feast together!"

After a moment of hesitation, we all walked up to the table. There was a ton of food! Everything from fruits and vegetables, to fish and steak. Even my favorite . . . fried chicken! The dishes were all silver and shiny. A dozen candles burned in golden candle holders. It was, as they say, a feast fit for a king!

Count Dracula remained standing at the head of the table, and I realized that he was waiting for us to sit. We pulled out our chairs and sat, and the Count followed.

"Yes, yes," he said. "It has been so long since I've had guests. I'm so happy you could join me."

"Where did all of this food come from?" Scott asked.

Count Dracula looked confused. "Why ... the kitchen, of course," he replied. "That's where all food comes from."

"Well, this is very nice of you, Mr. Dracula," Courtney said. "But what we really want is to go home. We have to find Jeffrey. Do you know where we might find him?"

The Count shook his head. "I'm afraid I don't know any 'Jeffrey'," he replied.

"Well, then, how about a way out? We have to find a door that leads back to our home in Missouri."

"Ah, yes," the Count replied, taking an ear of corn in his hands. "The door out. Yes, I'll take you there right after we eat."

He raised the ear of corn to his lips and opened his mouth. My jaw dropped and I felt a spasm of terror when I saw his long white fangs. I clutched my neck to protect it, then the next moment I felt silly. He bit into the ear of corn. He wasn't after my neck after all. In less than thirty seconds, he'd polished off every last kernel from the ear of corn.

"Really?" Tony said. "You know where the door is?"

"Of course," Count Dracula replied. "I've lived here for a long, long time. I know where everything is. Please . . . eat, and be my guests."

So . . . we ate. I stuffed myself on some of the best food I've ever had in my life. We all did. I hadn't realized how hungry I'd been, but come to think of it, we'd all gone a long time without eating.

After we ate, Count Dracula stood. "My friends—thank you," he said. "I am so pleased that you have been my guests. Now, I will be happy to show you this 'door' that you're looking for."

"Cool," Scott said.

The Count turned, glided toward the wall, and stood before an old picture.

"My great-great-great grandfather, Count Poindexter," he said, staring up at the painting.

I giggled, and Dracula turned and stared at me.

"I'm sorry," I said, hiding my smile with my hand. "It's just that . . . well . . . 'Poindexter' sounds like a funny name for a vampire."

"Ah, yes," the Count replied. "Many vampires made fun of him. But he was a kind, kind, man."

"You said that you were going to show us the door," Courtney said.

"Of course, of course," Count Dracula replied.

He reached out his arms, grasped the painting from both sides, and lifted it from the wall. Behind the painting—

Was a door!

"It has been hidden here a long time," Dracula said. "I, of course, am not allowed to travel through it. But there it is. It will take you to where you want to go."

Because the door was actually in the wall and off the ground, we'd all need to stand on a chair to go through. Scott pulled over a chair from the dining table and placed it near the wall, below the door.

"I'll go first," Tony said, and he stepped up and onto the chair. The door had no handle, so he just pushed one side of it. The door swung open easily, but, just like the other doors we had traveled through, there was nothing to see on the other side.

"Thanks for the dinner, Count," Tony said, and he climbed through the open door and vanished.

"Yeah, thanks," Courtney said, and she, too, stepped onto the chair and climbed through the door. Scott followed, and I was last.

"See ya," I said.

"Be well," the Count replied.

I pulled myself up and climbed through the door, wondering just where we were going to end up this time.

26

Suddenly, I found myself standing in bright sunshine. Scott, Tony, and Courtney were at my side, and they were gazing at our new surroundings.

The castle no longer existed. Neither did the door. I turned to look, but it was gone.

"I think we're home!" Courtney exclaimed. "This sure looks a lot like Blue Springs to me!"

And it did.

We were in a large field. Around the field, tall trees grew. The sky was blue and blotted with fluffy, white clouds. A typical day in Missouri.

"Yes, this *does* look like home," Scott said. "But I don't recognize anything. I don't know where we are."

"Well, we could start walking until we find a road or something," I said.

Tony shook his head. "No," he said. "I think we ought to wait a minute. I don't think this is where you live. Remember . . . there are lots of different realms in the house."

"But where, then?" I asked. "Where do you think we are?"

"I'm not sure, but—"

Suddenly, he stopped speaking.

"What's the—" Scott began to say, but Tony interrupted.

"Shhhhh!" he said. "Listen!"

We listened for a moment. I didn't hear anything.

"What is it?" Courtney asked. "What did you hear?"

And suddenly, I heard a noise. A distant rumble, like a train. It grew louder and louder.

"What's that?" Scott asked.

Tony shook his head and continued looking around. "I'm not sure," he replied, "but it sounds like it might be—"

"*LOOK!*" Courtney cried, thrusting her arm into the air and pointing.

On the other side of the field was a terrifying sight.

"*Oh my gosh!*" I exclaimed.

The four of us stood, completely frozen by fear.

On the other side of the field was the biggest, blackest, ugliest tornado I could ever imagine. Its terrible winds spun in a circular fashion, and lighting bolts pierced its sides. On the ground, trees snapped like twigs.

And the tornado was headed right for us!

27

"Run for your lives!" Tony screamed. *"It's headed right for us!"*

The roaring sound was growing louder by the second. I watched, horrified, as the monster tornado ripped a tree from the ground and threw it into the sky like a toy. Other trees were whipping and cracking, and several more were pulled out, roots and all, and sent churning into the air.

"We've got to find a ditch!" Scott screamed. *"We've got to find some place to get out of the wind!"*

The four of us took off, running as fast as we could, away from the howling tornado. I knew there was no way we would be able to outrun the sinister funnel cloud, and our only hope would be to get out of its direct path. I learned in school that if you were ever caught outside in a tornado, it was best to find a ditch or a low area, lay flat on your stomach, and cover your head with your hands.

Problem was, we didn't know if there was any ditch nearby!

We left the field and entered the woods. All around us, the trees were bending and twisting. I knew the tornado was getting closer.

"We aren't going to make it!" Courtney shrieked.

"Yes we are!" Scott shouted back. "There's a small ditch up ahead! Run faster!"

I looked up ahead. Among the swaying trees I could make out a dry creek bed. If we could make it there, we might have a chance.

"Faster, Courtney!" I urged. "We're almost there!"

The wind whipped me sideways, and I knew that the tornado was almost upon us. The sky darkened, and I heard tree limbs snapping and breaking. A big branch fell right next to me!

Ahead, I saw Tony and Scott dive into the ditch. Courtney and I followed close behind, and we dove in just in time. The four of us lay on our stomachs, covering our heads.

"It's coming!" Scott shouted.

I turned my head in time to see the ugliest black cloud I have ever seen in my life. It was whirling and whipping about, faster than I've ever seen a cloud move before. Whole trees were being uprooted and tossed about. It was terrifying . . . and it was going to pass right over top of us!

28

The roaring became unbearable. It sounded like the space shuttle blasting off right next to me! I heard someone yell something, but I couldn't tell who it was, even though the voice was right next to me.

And suddenly—it was upon us. Sand and dirt ripped against my skin, and I kept my eyes closed really tight. My hair felt like it was being torn from my head.

Now I know what Dorothy felt like in the Wizard of Oz!

I felt myself being pulled from the ground, and I tried to grab something—anything—to hold onto, but there was nothing to grasp. The tornado was pulling at me, and I struggled and fought to stay on the ground.

But it was no use. I heard a scream, and out of the corner of my eye I saw Courtney go flying up into the air!

My hands dug into the dirt, desperately trying to find something to hold, but it was no use. The wind was too strong, too powerful—and in the next instant, I was torn from the ground and yanked up into the air! This was worse than my most terrible nightmare!

I screamed, but I couldn't even hear my own voice over the roar of the funnel cloud. I was flying, bolstered by the powerful wind, through the air and up into the sky.

I don't know how long I was carried in the air like that. Everything had happened so fast. I couldn't see above, below, or around me. Everything was a dark, charcoal gray.

All of a sudden I was whipped sideways, and I went sailing in a different direction altogether. I heard Courtney scream, but I couldn't see her.

Then I realized something.

The tornado had carried us high into the sky. Now it had spit us out like cherry pits, and there was nowhere to go but down.

I shut my eyes, and realized that it was the end . . . for all of us.

29

I could feel it now. I could feel my body free falling, twisting and turning, end over end, plunging back to earth. There was simply no way we would survive.

I opened my eyes . . . and discovered that we were over water! Below me was what appeared to be an ocean, all shiny and blue. I could see land not far off, but the important thing was that it looked like I was going to land in the water!

And Courtney was below me! She was screaming her head off, louder than I'd ever heard her scream before. Scott was in the air, too, and so was Tony!

The wind rushed past, and I shouted to Courtney.

"Stop your screaming! Save your breath for when you land in the water!"

Courtney stopped screaming. She tumbled head over heels, and I caught a glimpse of her face. She was terrified, just like the rest of us.

Would we survive hitting the water? Sure, the water would be softer than hitting the ground, but we were high in the air. Courtney has a pool at her house with a diving board high in the air. We jump off it all the time . . . but it's only eight feet in the air.

Right now, we were falling from more than a hundred feet!

Beneath us, the surface of the water was rushing closer and closer. In a matter of seconds, we would splash down.

I took a deep breath and held it. I was sure that I would need it.

Then I had another thought:

What if there are sharks in the water, like we saw in the river? Then what?

I looked all around, but I didn't see any sharks.

Below me, Courtney was flailing her arms like crazy. We were only seconds from hitting the water.

"Take a deep breath!" I shouted to her. Then I took a deep breath, closed my eyes tightly . . . and prepared to hit the water.

30

When I hit the water, it felt like I was hitting bricks. I was disoriented, underwater. Water went up my nostrils and I blew it out. I flailed my arms around, and suddenly —

I broke the surface!

I coughed and sputtered, and spit out the water I had swallowed. A few feet away, Courtney was doing the same.

Then we heard two huge splashes as Scott and Tony hit the water. They disappeared beneath the surface for a moment, then popped back up.

We were alive! We made it!

"Courtney! Amber!" Scott shouted. "Are you guys okay?"

"I'm fine," I said.

"Me too," Courtney replied with a cough. "I think I swallowed ten gallons of water, though!"

Land was a few hundred feet away, and we all started swimming toward it. I was still nervous, thinking there might be sharks around, but I didn't see any.

In a few minutes we reached the sandy beach and crawled up onto dry land. Palm trees swayed lazily, and the sky was crystal blue. I was sure that we were in Florida or Hawaii or somewhere in the tropics.

"I can't believe that so many things can happen to four people in the same day," I said, shaking my head. "And it all started with that silly Madhouse."

"Don't forget," Tony said, "we're still in the Madhouse. We are in the different realms contained within it."

"I hope nobody else comes into the house," Courtney said. "So far, we've been pretty lucky. Other people might not be."

But I had been wondering something. Tony seemed to know a lot about where we were going . . . sometimes. Other times, he had no clue where we were. I decided to ask him.

"Say, Tony . . . have you been here before?"

"Yeah, I think so," he said, looking around. "Why?"

"Well, you act like you know your way around sometimes. Other times you seem completely lost."

Tony hung his head. "You're right," he said. "I don't exactly know how to get out."

"But you said you were going to take us to Jeffrey!" Scott said. "You said Jeffrey is a wizard, and he knows how we can get out."

"I don't think Jeffrey wants you to leave," Tony said. "See . . . Jeffrey is really lonely. That's why he created all of this. So he would have friends to enjoy it. That's why it's so hard to find him."

"When I see Jeffrey, I'm going to give him a piece of my mind!" Courtney fumed. "My mom and dad are probably worried sick. We've been gone a long time!"

Tony shook his head. "No. All time has stopped here. When you return to your world, you will realize that no time has gone by at all."

"If we get back to our world," I said.

"You will," Tony replied hopefully. "I think I know how to get back."

"I hope so," Scott said, and I could tell by the way he said it that he wasn't real happy.

Tony pointed. "I think there's a river over there, not far," he said. "We'll follow it up until we come to another door."

"Yeah . . . and what's going to happen to us on the way to the door?" I said.

"Nothing," Tony said. "I promise. There's nothing to be worried about."

It was a promise that Tony wouldn't be able to keep, because there was plenty we had to worry about . . . more so than we could possibly imagine.

31

Sure enough, after walking for a few minutes, we came to a river. It was deep and wide, and edged with all different kinds of trees that I'd never seen before. At least not in Missouri, anyway.

"Let's follow the river upstream," Tony said, pointing. "I think there's a door not far away."

"Will Jeffrey be there?" I asked.

"Yeah, I think so," Tony said. "I think he will be."

We walked and walked. It was really hot, and pretty soon we were all sweating.

"I hope I don't get a sunburn," Courtney said. "I'm not wearing any sun screen."

"You could have bigger problems," I said. "We were lucky to get away from that tornado."

"Yeah, you're right," she said. "I'll just be glad when we get back home."

We continued walking as the sun beat down upon us.

"It's not much farther," Tony said. "I think it's only a half-mile or so up the river."

"I'm tired," I said. "Let's stop for a moment and rest."

And that's what we did. I sat in the shade of a palm tree, and Courtney sat next to me. Tony went on ahead, and Scott went to the river's edge to splash water on his face.

"Do you think Tony really knows where he's going?" Courtney asked.

I shook my head. "I have no idea. But he says he's been here before. He seems to know his way around a little."

"He just seems a little strange. Oh, he seems like a nice enough person, but he just seems a little odd."

"I'm sure it will all make sense soon," I said hopefully, "as soon as we find Jeffrey."

"I hope you're right," Courtney said.

"I am. Come on . . . let's cool off down by the river."

We stood and began walking to where Scott was on the bank of the river. He was kneeling by the water, splashing water in his face.

Which meant that there was no way he could see what Courtney and I were seeing.

In the water, right in front of Scott, was a huge crocodile! Its head was bigger than a watermelon, and its eyes were staring at the human shape kneeling at the edge of the river.

Then suddenly, without warning, the crocodile opened it huge jaws . . . *and attacked!*

32

"Scott!" I screamed.

Scott dropped his hands from his face just in time to see the gigantic reptile lunging.

"Aaahhhh!" Scott screamed, and he sprang to his feet, spun, and fled.

But the crocodile was faster. It lunged forward, and with a mighty snap of its powerful jaws, it clamped down . . . narrowly missing Scott's foot!

Scott ran, lickety-split, across the sand to where we stood. The crocodile, unsuccessful, slunk back into the water, then vanished beneath the surface.

"That was . . .was . . . just . . . just too close," Scott panted. "I thought that thing was going to get me for sure!"

"We did, too," Courtney said, trying to calm her own rapidly-beating heart.

I saw a movement upstream, and Tony appeared.

"Hey guys!" he shouted, waving his arm. "I found it! I found the door!"

"Maybe we're going to get out of here after all," Scott said.

"Yeah, well, let's just wait and see before we get our hopes up," Courtney replied. Then she glanced at her bare arms. "I can tell already that I'm going to have a bad sunburn."

"Come on!" Tony urged, and the three of us began walking toward him.

"How can you be sure we're not just going to get into a whole bunch more trouble?" Scott asked, when we'd reached Tony. "I mean . . . where is this door going to take us?"

"I can't say for sure . . . but I think it is a door that will lead out. Really."

We didn't have much choice. It was either go through the door, or spend the rest of our lives on the lookout for crocodiles.

"It's this way," Tony said, and we followed him.

Just as he said, we found the door. Again, it looked like the rest of the doors we had encountered. It was just a door, standing alone. There were no walls, nothing. I walked all around it, even on the other side, to see what was there.

Nothing. That's all it was.

A door.

"Well," I said, "let's try it again. I wonder where we're going to end up."

Tony reached out and grasped the doorknob.

"Ready?" he said.

Scott, Courtney, and I nodded.

"Here goes," he said, and he pushed the door open. Again, there was nothing to see but fuzzy black. It sure looked strange, this door that opened into another world.

Tony took a step through, and vanished.

"Let's all three go at the same time," I said, taking Courtney's hand. Scott grasped my other hand, and we all took a breath, and stepped through.

And in a split-second, I knew that we'd made our biggest mistake yet.

33

Instantly, our bodies went into shock from the gripping, burning cold. We went from being hot and sweaty to being frozen stiff. Wind howled at my ears, and my face felt like ice.

We were in a raging blizzard!

"Oh, this is g . . . g . . . great!" Courtney shrieked. "We go from hot sun to a snowstorm! We're going to freeze to death!"

"Sorry, guys," Tony apologized. "I thought this door was the way out. I really did."

"N . . . n . . . now what d . . . d . . . do we . . . d . . . do?" I stammered. I was already shivering, and I knew that the four of us wouldn't last long in this kind of weather. Not without a coat, or mittens, or hats.

"We have to keep moving," Scott said. "We have to keep moving or else we'll freeze."

"I think we're al . . . al . . . already f . . . f . . . freezing," I said. "But you're right. Let's get moving."

It was hard to walk. Snow had piled up over a foot high, which meant that we had to lift our feet up to take each step. It was very tiring.

But I wasn't worried about being tired. I was worried about the cold. If we didn't find shelter, or a way out, we weren't going to last long. Soon, we'd all have frostbite, and become walking ice cubes.

Then, we would just be ice cubes . . . frozen solid.

Suddenly, Scott stopped and pointed. "What's that?!?!" he exclaimed.

"It b . . . better . . . n . . . not b . . . b . . . be a shark, or a t . . . tornado, or a c . . . croc . . . crocodile," Courtney stammered.

"It's not! Look!"

Through the blinding snow, we could make out a dark shape. It was about twice the size of a football, perched waist-high.

"What is it?" I asked.

"I'm not sure," Scott replied. "B . . . but it looks . . . looks . . . like . . . like . . . like a m . . . m . . . mail . . . b . . . .b . . . box!"

We walked closer, and sure enough — it *was* a mailbox! Here in the middle of a blizzard, wherever we were, we had found a mailbox!

But that wasn't the most amazing part. The most amazing part was when we saw the name written on the side of the mailbox.

That was unbelievable.

All four of us read in unison what was written on the mailbox.

"*S. Claus?!?!*"

The wind howled and the snow whipped at our faces, but for a moment, we forgot how cold it was.

"That's impossible!" Scott said.

"It can't be!" Tony said.

"It's got to be!" I said. "We must be at the north pole!"

"Well, if *that's* Santa Claus's m . . . m . . . mailbox, then where d . . . d . . . does he live?" Courtney stammered.

We all looked around, but in the blinding snow, we couldn't see anything but white.

Tony inspected the mailbox. "Well, the door opens this way," he said, "so I would imagine that Santa's house is down that way."

That made sense. But in the blizzard, we couldn't see any house or even a driveway.

"Let's go," Scott said, "before we freeze to death."

We hurried off in the direction where we thought Santa's house might be. I still couldn't believe it, but, then again, everything that had happened since we entered the madhouse had been unbelievable.

Soon, we could make out the shadow of a building through the thick snow.

"There it is!" Scott cried out. "It's Santa's house! It really is!"

We ran faster, and stopped at the front of the home. It was huge! It was built from logs, and there was a large stone chimney on top. On the front door were two giant candy cane decorations, and a sign that read:

MR. & MRS. S. CLAUS

"See?" Scott said. "We're really here! We're at the north pole!"

I wasn't going to wait any longer. I ran up to the front door and rang the doorbell. I was freezing, and I needed to get warm fast.

There was no answer, and I rang the doorbell again. I waited.

Scott, Tony, and Courtney joined me. Soon we were all banging on the door and ringing the doorbell.

"Mr. Claus!" I shouted. "Mr. Claus? Are you home?"

"Maybe he's out taking care of the reindeer," Scott said.

"In *this* weather?" I replied.

"Mr. Claus!" Tony shouted.

And suddenly — the door opened.

But whoever opened the door was definitely *not* Santa Claus . . . .

35

When the door suddenly swung open, all four of us jumped.

"May I help you?" a tiny voice asked . . . but I couldn't see anyone! Not at first, anyway. Then I realized that the person that had opened the door was very, very short . . . not even half as big as me! He had on blue overalls and a red and white striped shirt, and he was wearing a baseball cap with the words *ELF UNION LOCAL 482*.

"May I help you?" he asked again.

It was one of Santa's elves! It had to be!

"Ummm, yeah," Tony said. "We're here to see Mr. Claus."

"Do you have an appointment?"

"A *what?*" I asked.

"An appointment. Mr. Claus is very busy this time of year, you know. He just finished his list, and now he's checking it twice. It's a tough job."

"Can we come inside for a few minutes?" I asked. "Please? We're freezing, and we don't have any coats or hats or anything."

The elf looked up at us.

"Certainly," he replied. "Do come in and have a seat. I will see if Santa is available, but I doubt it."

The elf waddled away from the door and we stepped inside. It didn't look like a house at all. We were in a small room. There was a desk with a telephone, several chairs, a couch, and a small table with a bowl of candy canes. Behind the desk was a large, closed door, with a big sign on it with one word: *PRIVATE*

"Please, have a seat," the elf said. "I'll see if Mr. Claus will see you." Then he turned, walked behind the desk, opened the door with the *private* sign, and left. The door clicked closed, and the four of us were left alone.

Courtney and I sat on the couch. Scott and Tony each sat in a chair.

"*This is bizarre,*" I whispered to Courtney.

"*You're telling me,*" Courtney whispered back. "*I didn't even believe in Santa Claus!*"

"*You're kidding?!?!*" I replied. "*You don't believe in Santa Claus?!?!*"

"*I do now,*" Courtney said. "*Especially if I get a chance to actually meet him. I'm going to ask him for a puppy.*"

I rolled my eyes. "*How about we ask him to help us get home and out of this freaky madhouse?*" I suggested.

"*Well, yeah, that too,*" she agreed. "*Then I'm going to ask him for a puppy.*"

We waited for a few minutes. Suddenly, the door behind the desk opened, and the elf appeared.

"Mr. Claus will see you," the elf said. He waved us toward him. "Follow me, please."

We got up walked behind the desk, and followed the elf through the door.

Now we were in a big warehouse . . . and when I say *big* . . . I mean *big*. The place was *huge!*

Boxes and crates were stacked from the floor to the ceiling, and the ceiling had to be two hundred feet high!

"This must be where all of the toys are stored," Scott said.

We followed the elf through the warehouse until we came to another door. The elf opened it and we followed.

Now we were in a factory! There were machines and tools and conveyor belts and all kinds of gizmos everywhere . . . but none of them were working. And we didn't see any elves, either, which was strange. I thought that they'd be busy every single day of the year making toys and things.

"Where are all of the workers?" I asked.

Without turning around, the elf replied. "Union cookie break. All elves get a fifteen-minute milk and cookie break every three hours."

"Oh," I said.

We continued through the factory until we came to another door. A sign on the wall read:

Mr. S. Claus, Toy and Gift Purveyor.

"What's a 'purveyor'?" Courtney whispered.

"*Someone who supplies or deals in something,*" I whispered back.

"This is too cool," Scott said. "I haven't seen Santa since I was at the mall last Christmas!"

The elf tapped lightly on the door. "Mr. Claus?" he said. "Your guests are here."

The door opened slowly, and there, in the flesh, stood Santa Claus . . . but he didn't look anything like the Santa Claus that I knew!

36

Santa Claus stood in the doorway.

"Welcome, friends," he boomed. His voice was deep and gravelly, just like I remembered it. He was a large man, too . . . just like I remembered him to be.

But he didn't have a beard! Or even white hair! His hair was dark brown and short. He wore a blue pinstripe suit and a yellow tie. He looked more like a businessman that Santa Claus!

Scott noticed the difference, too. "Mr. Claus, you sure look different from the last time I saw you."

"Of course I do, Scott," Santa replied.

"You . . . you remember my name?!?!" Scott stammered.

"Of course!" Santa replied. "That's my job. I know everyone's names and addresses, and I know if you've been naughty or nice."

"But . . . but why do you look like you do?" I asked. "Aren't you supposed to wear a red suit and boots? And you always have a beard."

"Oh, that's just for entertainment and marketing," Santa replied. "I need the red suit to keep me warm, of course, but the hair and the beard are strictly for show."

"You . . . you mean it's all an act?" Scott said.

Santa Claus shook his head. "Not at all," he replied. "But the wig and the beard get hot, and it's nice not to have to wear them all year long."

I hadn't thought about that.

"So, let's see," Santa continued. He looked at me. "Amber DeBarre. You've been very good this year."

"I have? I . . . I mean . . . yes . . . yes, I have been good."

"And Scott," Santa said, "you haven't been too bad. However, I want you to stop poking your sister in the ribs at the dinner table."

"You know about that?!?!" Scott exclaimed.

Santa nodded. "And I also know about the worm you put on your teacher's desk."

Scott looked horrified.

"However," Santa continued, "there's still time for you to turn things around before Christmas."

"I will," Scott said, nodding his head frantically. "I will! I promise, Mr. Claus!"

Santa turned and looked at Courtney. "And you, Miss Richards. You didn't even believe that I existed, did you?"

"Ummm . . . I ummm . . . no, I . . . I guess I didn't. But I do now!"

"Good. And I think you just might get that puppy you've wanted," he said with a wink.

Courtney's eyes lit up. "Really?!?!" she exclaimed. "Thank you, Santa, thank you! You're the best!"

But what happened next took Scott, Courtney and me by complete surprise.

Santa looked straight at Tony, pointed an accusing finger at him, and said:

"But you . . . you haven't been good at all this year, Jeffrey . . . "

37

Oh my gosh! Could it be? Was Tony not really 'Tony' at all? Was he really Jeffrey?

"Honest, Santa!" Tony/Jeffrey said. "I . . . I didn't mean anything!   I was just lonely and wanted some friends to hang out with!"

"You tricked these three young people into thinking that they couldn't go home," Santa said coldly.

"You did *what?!?!*" Courtney cried.

"It's true," Jeffrey said. He hung his head. "My name isn't Tony. I'm Jeffrey. I'm the wizard who created everything in the Missouri Madhouse."

"But . . . but how? Why?" I asked.

"I live in a different realm than you do. I can't go into your realm, but I found out a way to allow people to come into mine. You see, where I live, there are no other kids around. It's really boring. So I created the Madhouse . . . and everything in it, so people would come and have fun."

"So you're the boy that everyone has seen in the windows of the Madhouse!" I exclaimed.

Jeffrey nodded. "Yes, but I can't leave. That's why I need people to come to my realm."

"You can't keep people in your own world just because you want them to stay," Scott said. "Besides . . . they wouldn't like you if you did that."

"I realize that now," Jeffrey said, hanging his head.

"But how did you create everything?" I asked. "You created all of these different realms? You created Count Dracula and the giant ant and the sharks and the crocodile?"

"Yes," Jeffrey answered sheepishly. "You see, in my realm, where I live, I can create all of those places and things very easily. I guess you would call it 'magic,' but for me, it's just something that

I do to keep from being bored. I was born a wizard, and I'll always be one."

"But we could've been eaten alive by that giant ant and those sharks! We were almost wiped out by that tornado!" Courtney said.

Jeffrey shook his head. "No," he said. "We were never in any danger. None of those things would have actually hurt us. I only did it because I wanted some friends to hang out with. I'm sorry."

I know that what he had done was wrong, but I kind of felt bad for him. He must be really lonely.

"But wait a minute," Scott said. He looked up at Santa Claus. "If Jeffrey created all of the realms that we passed through, that means that he created you, too."

Santa shook his head. "No, I'm afraid Jeffrey's trickery just got out of hand. When I saw what was going on, I decided that I must put a stop to it. I was the one who created the door that brought you to the north pole."

"So, we're actually on earth, right?" I asked.

"Yes, you are," Santa replied. "You are a long way from Missouri, but you are on earth."

"So that means that time is going by!" Courtney said. "Isn't that right?"

"That's right," Santa answered.

"Man, we'd better get home!" Scott said.

"But how?" I said. "It's a blinding snowstorm outside!"

"Don't worry, don't worry," Santa replied. "Everything will work out fine. First things first." He turned to Jeffrey. "I want *you* to dismantle your madhouse. Allow everyone to go back to their own realms, if they want to. Especially the people at the carnival."

"I will," Jeffrey said.

"Good," said Santa. "You'll find that you must *earn* the friendship of others. You can't trick anyone into being your friend."

Jeffrey nodded.

"And as for you three," he said, "we need to get you home. Come with me."

We followed Santa as he walked through the factory. Many of the elves had finished with their milk and cookie break and were returning to their jobs.

At the far end of the factory was a window. Outside, the snow was still coming down like crazy. Santa walked to the window and opened it up. Cold air and snow blew inside.

"There you are," he said. "Home."

"Say what?" Courtney exclaimed. "Santa . . . we'll freeze to death!"

Santa smiled and shook his head. "No, you won't," he said. "Remember how you first entered the Madhouse?"

We all nodded.

"And so, this is how you will return to Missouri. Simply climb through the window."

It made sense. That's how we traveled to all of those other realms that Jeffrey had created. It was only logical that we would return home through a window.

"I'm really sorry I did what I did," Jeffrey said. "I hope you'll forgive me."

"I do," I said.

"Yeah, me too," said Courtney. "Only next time, don't try to trick us."

"I won't," Jeffrey said.

"I'll tell you what," Scott said. "We'll come and visit you once in a while. You know . . . just to hang out."

Jeffrey's eyes lit up. "Really?" he said. "You mean it?"

We all nodded. "Sure," I said.

"That would be great!" he exclaimed.

"We've got to get going," Scott said, and he walked up to the window. "You know, this has actually been kind of cool. I had fun, I guess."

And with that, Scott slipped through the open window . . . and vanished. Courtney was next, and she, too, vanished the moment she went out the window.

"See you later," I said as I approached the window.

"Good-bye," Jeffrey and Santa said.

I climbed through the window, thinking that I would immediately be back in Blue Springs, on the porch of the Madhouse.

But that's not what happened. What happened was totally unexpected, so horrifying, that I knew Santa had made a big mistake.

I was suddenly spinning, out of control, through some kind of tunnel! Bright lights flashed all around, and it felt like I was riding an out-of-control roller coaster! I was twisting and turning, going faster and faster and faster, falling down a winding, narrow tube.

And Scott and Courtney were nowhere to be seen.

I tried to get some kind of control, but it was impossible. I just kept tumbling and turning.

Something must be wrong! I thought. *What if I wind up spinning in this tunnel forever?!?!*

I needn't have worried. Very soon, I began to feel my body slow down. I could see a light from up ahead, and as I drew nearer, I could see that it was a window. The light coming from the other side of the window was so bright I had to close my eyes.

Next thing I knew, I was through the window, where I landed in a big heap . . . right on top of Scott and Courtney! We were on the front porch of the Madhouse!

"Ouch!" Courtney cried out.

"Oof!" I said as I tumbled to the side.

"Man, that was freaky!" Scott exclaimed. "That was the best roller coaster ride I've ever been on in my life!"

"I'm just glad we're back in one piece," I said. I jumped to my feet and leapt off the porch. Then I turned around and looked up at the house.

It sure felt good to finally be home.

Suddenly, Courtney gasped. "Oh no!" she exclaimed. "My autograph! I forgot to get an autograph from Count Dracula!"

"If that's your biggest problem, you don't have much to worry about," I said.

"Yeah," she said. "I guess you're right."

The sun had set, and the sky was getting dark. It was time to go home.

"We'll see you later, Scott," I said. "Do you want to come back tomorrow and visit Jeffrey?"

"I've got to help my dad first, but if I have the time, I will."

"Good night," Courtney said.

We walked home, talking about everything that had happened to us. We still had a lot of questions for Jeffrey.

"I wonder where he lives?" I said. "I mean, I know he lives in a different realm, but where? And where are all of the people in the carnival from?"

"You've got me," Courtney replied. "Maybe tomorrow we can ask him."

When we got home, Mom was in the living room, reading a magazine.

"Hello, girls," she said. "Did you have a nice walk?"

I looked at Courtney and grinned. "Sort of," I said.

The next day, Courtney and I had breakfast and decided to go to the Madhouse to see if we could find Jeffrey. We had a lot of questions that we wanted to ask him. Plus, I felt kind of bad for him, since he seemed so lonely. I thought he might like it if we hung out with him for a while.

Besides . . . we really had a lot of fun at the carnival. I was looking forward to going on all of the rides again.

We walked up to the Madhouse. The sun was shining, and, even though the house looked old, it didn't seem to look as creepy as it had in the past.

Maybe it was because now we knew the secret.

We walked quickly up to the porch and up to the window. I couldn't wait to get back to the carnival!

The window was still open. "You want to go first?" Courtney asked.

"Sure," I replied, and I climbed through the open window.

But something was wrong.

The carnival was gone.

"Hey," I heard Courtney say. "You didn't disappear! You're still standing there!"

"Yeah," I replied, looking around. "The carnival is gone, too. It's just an old house."

"Do you think that Jeffrey made it go away?" Courtney asked.

I nodded sadly. "Yeah, probably. I guess I just hoped it would still be here."

Courtney climbed through the window and stood next to me.

"Jeffrey?" I called out. "Are you here?"

No answer.

"What's this?" Courtney said, and she bent over to pick up a piece of paper. She stood up and turned the paper over in his hands.

"It's a note from Jeffrey!" she exclaimed, and she began reading it out loud.

"Dear Friends:

I apologize again for tricking you into staying with me. I hope you understand. But a funny thing happened. After I dismantled all of my realms and let everyone go wherever they wanted, many of them decided to stay. Now I've got a ton of friends, and I promise not to bother you anymore. Thanks for showing me what good friends are all about."

"So, he's gone," I said sadly.

"Yeah, he is," Courtney replied. "But hey . . . at least he's happy."

"Yeah, I guess that's the important part."

We left the Madhouse and went home. Once in a while we would return and walk up to the window and look inside, but we never again saw anything strange. Matter of fact, the rest of summer was really boring . . . until I got a call from my cousin.

It was the week before school was supposed to start. I was getting ready for bed when my cousin Ryan called. He used to live in Missouri, but he and his sister and his mom and dad moved to Pennsylvania. He's really funny, and I miss him a lot.

"Hey Amber!" he exclaimed when I picked up the phone.

"Ryan!" I exclaimed. "How are you?"

"Well, I'm fine now," he said. "But I wasn't yesterday!"

"Why?" I replied.   "What happened yesterday?"

"Do you know what a python is?"

I thought about it. "Yeah," I answered. "It's a snake, isn't it?"

"Yeah," Ryan said. "Well, you're going to freak when I tell you what happened!"

I laughed, because I knew that whatever he told me about pythons couldn't be any freakier than what happened to Courtney, Scott, and me in the Missouri Madhouse.

But then he began his story, and I realized that I was wrong. What happened to Ryan was a lot freakier than what happened to me.

In fact, it was *terrifying* . . . .

next in the

AMERICAN CHILLERS

SERIES:

#11:

POISONOUS

PYTHONS

PARALYZE

PENNSYLVANIA

**turn the page to read a few
chilling chapters!**

1

"See anything yet?" I called out.

"Nothing yet," I heard a voice in the woods reply. The voice belonged to my friend Stephen Kottler, and we'd been hunting for garter snakes in the woods near our house. So far, we hadn't found anything, and I was about to give up.

My name is Ryan Brindley, and I live in Maple Glen. It's a city in Pennsylvania, not far from Philadelphia. We used to live in Missouri, but we moved here a few years ago when Mom changed jobs. I really like it here. There are lots of forests and trees, but best of all . . . garter snakes.

Garter snakes are my favorite kind of snake. First of all, you can find them just about anywhere. They are black with a yellow stripe down their back, and they have a creamy yellow belly. Plus, they're pretty much harmless. Oh, I caught a lot of garter snakes when I lived in Missouri, but I catch more here.

We don't really do anything with the snakes, either. I used to think that it would be cool to have one as a pet, but you can't keep a wild snake. I think it's more fun just to catch a snake and watch it for a while . . . and then let it go.

My friend Stephen loves to catch snakes, too, and so does our friend Heather Lewis. I used to think that girls didn't like snakes, but Heather does, and she's good at catching them, too. Today, she had soccer practice, so she couldn't be with us.

And normally, we all have a lot of fun.

Normally.

But today, we were going to discover something that would turn things in our entire city upside down.

"Let's hunt in the swamp," I suggested, and pretty soon I saw Stephen appear from the woods. His blonde hair shined in the afternoon sun, and his face was damp with sweat.

"Yeah, let's try the swamp," he agreed. "I haven't seen a single snake."

The swamp isn't far from where we live. It's dense and thick, and it's hard to walk through.

We had just entered the swamp, and I was right behind Stephen when he suddenly stopped.

"Shhh," he said. "I think I heard something."

Quietly, I stepped up to his side. We listened. All we could hear were a few birds chirping, and the sound of a small airplane way up in the sky.

And suddenly—

We heard it.

The crackling, swishing sounds that a snake makes as it moves through brush and branches.

But this sound was different, somehow. It sounded . . .

Heavier.

Bigger.

If it was a snake, it was a big one.

My heart pounded. *"I think it's over there somewhere,"* I said, raising my arm to point.

Carefully, we took a few steps forward.

"There!" Stephen pointed. "I saw something move!"

We sprang, not knowing that what we were about to find was just some ordinary garter snake.

Now, I'm not afraid of snakes.

Period.

But the snake I saw at that moment was *horrifying*.

2

My heart stopped. Well, not really . . . but that's what it felt like. Stephen screamed and I thought he was going to faint.

It was a snake, all right . . . but it was like no snake I had ever seen in my life.

First of all, it was *big*. Longer than a car. It had splotches of different colors: green, gray, brown, and black.

And it was as big around as a football.

We couldn't move. I was too afraid to do anything, and so was Stephen. There was no way we were going to even *think* about catching this snake.

And besides . . . it's not smart to catch just any snake you see. Some of them bite, but I've found that if you leave them alone, they'll leave you alone. But it's not a good idea to just catch any snake that you come across. That's just asking for trouble.

"What . . . what kind of snake is that?" Stephen answered.

"It looks like some kind of boa constrictor," I answered quietly. *"But I can't be sure."*

"But there aren't any boa constrictors in Maple Glen, let alone Pennsylvania!" Stephen said.

The snake wasn't doing much, and it didn't seem to pay much attention to us. Finally, after a few more moments, it slowly slithered off into the swamp. The snake was gone.

"That was too cool!" I shouted after the snake had disappeared.

"That was awesome!" Stephen cried. "I've never seen a snake that big in my life!"

It was really kind of cool to see a snake like that, so close to home.

But something really bothered me.

That snake, whatever it was, wasn't from Pennsylvania. True, there are several kinds of snakes in our state—but none that grow to the size of the snake we'd seen in the swamp.

Later, when I got home, I looked through all of my snake books. I tried to find the name of the snake we'd spotted. I have lots of books on snakes, and I read all about them all the time.

But I couldn't find this snake in any of my books. I found a lot that looked like it, but I couldn't find the *exact* snake.

So I decided that I would go back into the swamp and see if I could find the snake again. I knew that Stephen would want to go, too.

I went to bed and fell asleep, not knowing that the very next day would lead to a discovery—a discovery that everyone in Maple Glen and even the entire state of Pennsylvania—would never forget.

3

I got up early the next morning and made preparations. I placed a couple of my snake books in my backpack, along with a first-aid kit, a ball of string, some mosquito repellant, and a compass—just in case we got lost in the swamp.

Then I rode my bike over to Stephen's house. He only lives a few blocks away.

Stephen was waiting in the garage. He had a backpack, too . . . but he was carrying bottles of water and sandwiches that his mom had made for us.

"All set?" I asked.

"Let's go snake hunting!" he said excitedly.

Our plan was to ride down to a small park that bordered on the edge of the swamp. From there, we could enter the swamp quickly without having to hike though the forest. Plus, we would ride right past Heather Lewis's house. I'm sure she would want to go with us today!

We stopped at her house and rang the doorbell. The door opened, and her mother appeared.

"Hi Mrs. Lewis," I said. "Is Heather around?"

"I'm afraid she's visiting her grandparents," Mrs. Lewis said. "But she'll be home later. I'll let her know you stopped by."

"Wait until she finds out what she missed!" Stephen said as we hopped on our bikes and rode out the driveway.

"I sure hope we see that monster snake again," I said.

We rode down the block. In no time at all, we were at the park. We locked our bikes up around a tree.

"Time to find us a snake," I said as we entered the swamp.

"A *giant* snake!" Stephen chimed.

"With *huge* teeth!" I exclaimed

"And dark, beady eyes!" Stephen said.

We were excited, to be sure.

But after hours and hours of scouring the swamp, we hadn't seen any evidence of the enormous snake. I caught one garter snake, and I let him go after a few minutes.

But that was all.

At noon, we decided to split up. We'd have a better chance finding the snake if we could each cover a little more ground. Every few minutes we would call out, just to make sure that we didn't get too far away from each other.

Branches scratched at my face. My muscles ached. Mosquitos nipped at my arm, even though I had bug spray on.

Man, I thought. *There is no way we're going to find that thing.*

I was bummed. I was really hoping that we'd see the snake again, but I knew that our chances were slim.

And suddenly. . . .

"HOLY COW!"

Stephen's voice pierced the swamp.

"Are you okay?" I called out frantically.

"Ryan! Get over here! You've got to see this!"

"Is it the snake?" I yelled back. I was already headed in his direction, sweeping branches and limbs out of my way.

"You're not going to believe this!" Stephen shouted. *"You're going to freak out!"*

And when I arrived at his side, I gasped.

Stephen was wrong.

When I saw what he'd found, I didn't just freak out.

I went bananas.

4

Stephen had found a snake skin.

Not just any snake skin.

An *enormous* snake skin.

You see, every once in a while, a snake will shed its skin. It rubs up against branches and brush, and the old skin gets caught. Then it kind of wriggles out, leaving behind a skin that is thin, like plastic. The shed skin is usually a creamy, light-brown color. It dries and becomes very brittle, but what it looks like, really, is the ghost of the snake. You can see the texture of scales on the skin and everything. I've found a few snake skins over the summer.

But none like this one.

Stephen and I just stared. The snake skin that we'd found must have been from the snake we saw the day before, because the skin was *huge*.

"I can't believe it!" Stephen whispered.

"Man, Heather is going to be sorry she missed finding this!" I said.

But we also knew something else:

The snake, wherever he was, might be dangerous.

"We have to tell someone," I said.

"Who?" Stephen replied. "The police?"

"No," I said, shaking my head. "We have to tell someone who knows about snakes. Someone who might know what kind of snake this is."

"But who?" Stephen said, scratching his head.

We thought and thought about it. The entire time, we didn't take our eyes off the giant snake skin.

All of a sudden, I knew who we could talk to.

"The pet store!" I exclaimed. "They have all kinds of different animals, including snakes! I'll bet the guy who runs the pet store would know what kind of snake this is!"

"Good idea!" Stephen replied. "But how are we going to get this skin out of here?"

"We're not," I said. "We'll leave it here. We'll bring the owner of the pet store out here to see it."

"Suppose we can't find it again?" Stephen asked.

"I've already got that one figured out," I said, as I slipped my backpack off. I unzipped it and pulled out the ball of string. "See? I'll tie this string onto this branch—"

As I spoke, I wound the white thread around a small sapling.

"—and I'll just let it out as we walk back. When we come back, all we have to do is follow the string. It'll lead us right to the snake skin!"

"Ryan, you're a genius!" Stephen shouted, and he raised his hand in the air. I slapped it and bowed.

"Yes, I am, aren't I?" I said with a smirk. "Come on. If we hurry, we can get to the pet store before it closes."

We backtracked through the swamp. All the while, I was letting out string so that we could follow it right back to the snake skin.

And I couldn't wait to tell the pet store owner! I was sure he'd be excited to see it.

Going back through the swamp was just as difficult as it was coming in. In many places the brush is so thick that you can't even see your shoes. Still, we pressed on, pushing branches and limbs out of our way as we moved forward.

We were almost out of the swamp. I was excited to go to the pet store and tell the owner about what we had found. He would know more about the snake skin, I was sure.

And so, I wasn't really paying attention to where I was walking. I was thinking about giant snakes and snake skins and—

Suddenly, I felt two sharp pains in my lower leg. It hurt! I screamed and tried to get away, but it was already too late. . . .

FUN FACTS ABOUT MISSOURI:

State Capitol: Jefferson City

State Mineral: Galena

State Nickname: The 'Show Me' State

State Song: "Missouri Waltz"

State Bird: Bluebird

State Motto: "The Welfare of the People shall be the Supreme Law"

State Tree: Flowering Dogwood

State Insect: honeybee

State Flower: Hawthorne

Statehood: August 10, 1821 (24th state)

FAMOUS MISSOURI PEOPLE!

Daniel Boone, hunter, trapper, trail-blazer

Dale Carnegie, motivational speaker and writer

Samuel L. Clemens, aka 'Mark Twain', humorist and writer *(One of Johnathan Rand's favorite authors!)*

Walt Disney, animator and movie maker

Jesse James, infamous outlaw and bandit

Harry S. Truman, judge, senator, president

Laura Ingalls Wilder, writer and pioneer

Harold Bell Wright, author

Kathleen Turner, actress

among many, many more!

Also by Johnathan Rand:

GHOST IN THE GRAVEYARD

About the author

Johnathan Rand is the author of the best-selling **'Chillers'** series, now with over 1,000,000 copies in print. In addition to the **'Chillers'** series, Rand is also the author of **'Ghost in the Graveyard'**, a collection of thrilling, original short stories featuring *The Adventure Club*. (And don't forget to check out **www.ghostinthegraveyard.com** and read an **entire story** from 'Ghost in the Graveyard' ***FREE!***) When Mr. Rand and his wife are not traveling to schools and book signings, they live in a small town in northern lower Michigan with their two dogs, Abby and Salty. He still writes all of his books in the wee hours of the morning, and still submits all manuscripts by mail. He is currently working on his newest series, entitled **'American Chillers'**. His popular website features hundreds of photographs, stories, and art work. Visit:

www.americanchillers.com

Join the official

AMERICAN CHILLERS

FAN CLUB!

Visit www.americanchillers.com for details!

For information on personal appearances,
motivational speaking engagements, or book
signings, write to:

AudioCraft Publishing, Inc.
PO Box 281
Topinabee Island, MI 49791

or call
(231) 238-0297

About the cover art: This unique cover was designed and created by Michigan artists Darrin Brege and Mark Thompson.

Darrin Brege works as an animator by day, and is now applying his talents on the internet, creating various web sites and flash animations. He attended animation school in southern California in the early nineties, and over the years has created original characters and animations for Warner Bros (Space Jam), for Hasbro (Tonka Joe Multimedia line), Universal Pictures (Bullwinkle and Fractured Fairy Tales CD Roms), and Disney. Besides art, he and his wife Karen are improv performers featured weekly at Mark Ridley's Comedy Castle over the last eight years. Improvisational comedy has provided the groundwork for a successful voice over career as well. Darrin has dozens of characters and impersonations in his portfolio. Darrin and Karen have a son named Mick.

Mark Thompson has been a professional illustrator for 25 years. He has applied his talents with toy companies Hasbro and Mattel, along with creating art for automobile companies. His work has been seen from San Diego Seaworld to Kmart stores, as well as the Detroit Tigers and the renowned 'Screams' ice-cream parlor in Hell, Michigan. Mark currently is designing holiday crafts for a local company, as well as doing website design and digital art from his home studio. He loves sci-fi and monster art, and also collects comics for a hobby. He has two boys of his own, and they're BIG Chiller Fans!

All AudioCraft books are proudly printed, bound, and manufactured in the United States of America, utilizing American resources, labor, and materials.

USA